勢覇

INTRODUCTION
THE STAGE IS SET

On the seventeenth floor of a tall, grey, glass encased skyscraper in the City of Los Angeles, a pretty, pale skinned, young woman kneels in the center of a ten by ten windowless room. She is naked and her hands are intertwined behind her head, her elbows up, causing her ample breasts to rise prominently on her chest. She has long, straight, black hair that descends to just below her shoulder blades. Her knees are spread wide, exposing the pale white, tender skin of her inner thighs, and the outer lips of her hairless sex. The floor is covered by a thin, light blue, rubberized mat. Next to her, along the wall, is a rolled up futon, a small locked chest, a plastic bottle of water and a covered chamber pot. A small desk-like, free standing platform sits in the corner of the room behind her. It is about two feet high, perfect for someone kneeling before it to write on. On the platform is a 5"x8" piece of ivory colored writing paper and an addressed envelope, both covered with the graceful lines of a woman's handwriting, and a pen. In the other corner is a 3'x3', empty, steel cage.

The girl is trembling, her inviting breasts quaking softly. Her long, wide nipples are taut and distended. There is a thick, black leather collar around the lithesome young woman's neck with gold colored rings at the front and back and similar bracelets around her ankles and wrists. A single drop of perspiration runs down the woman's right side, rolling slowly down her slender and shapely torso and dissipating as it reaches her right hip. It is clear that the woman is expecting someone, someone that she fears.

A slight moan escapes from the young woman's pursed lips. She has been holding this pose for an hour and her arms have become increasingly heavy, causing a deep, burning ache in her shoulders. The remnants of long, pink trails of abused skin suggest the reasons for the woman's trepidation. The faded lash marks cover her breasts and her flat, taut belly as well as the pale white skin of her rear and thighs. If one could see her back, one would see fresher, angrier red marks, the results of a recent whipping with a thin, leather covered reed, spread across it. The woman is breathing slowly, almost rhythmically, purposefully, as if preparing herself for an ordeal to come.

She shudders when she hears the sound of the handle of the door to her small prison turning. She has been staring at it for over an hour, anticipating its movement. Nonetheless, when it does move, it startles her.

A tall, heavy set man of obvious Asian descent steps into the room. He is wearing a bright green and red silk flowered kimono which accentuates his broad chest and the narrow grace of his hips. His legs are thick and long and he is wearing woven, straw sandals on his feet. His hair is jet black, like the girl's, but is cut short. There is no hair on his hard, square jaw or above his thin upper lip. The door closes behind the man and he places a plastic key card in the pocket of his kimono. To exit the tiny cell, one needs both the key card and the combination to the heavy, push button lock that seals the door shut. The combination is changed daily.

The man looks down on the kneeling, trembling woman. He takes the time to admire her luscious form and to enjoy the outer signs of her fear. In his right hand he is carrying the same thin, leather covered reed that has marked the young girl's back. He utters a sharp, one word command to the girl as he loosens the belt to his kimono and pulls it open. It is a command that the girl understands completely although she does not know the literal meaning of the word. She inches forwards on her knees, keeping her arms raised and her hands interlocked behind her head. Kneeling, with her back straight and erect, her mouth is just above the level of the helmeted head of the Asian man's long, limp cock. She has to bend her neck slightly to capture it between her lips.

Edging closer to the Asian man on her knees, the young woman wraps her plump, red lips around the thickening meat. She massages the man's tool with her tongue, encouraging it to hardness. The man gives out a low sigh as the hot moisture of the girl's mouth causes a wave of pleasure to flow through him.

Once the cock has hardened to its full length and thickness, the woman, known here only as Number 7, drags her lips slowly up and down its length. She knows that if she fails to pay proper obeisance to the man's pleasure she will surely feel the bite of the leather crop he still holds in his right hand. She forces her head forward until the head of the cock passes the entry to her throat. She coughs, slightly, as she fights off her body's rejection of this invasive flesh. The man has placed his hands on her head and, by his mere gentle pressure, keeps it positioned, the girl's face crushed against his loins. The young woman groans as the need for oxygen begins to become urgent. But the hands keep her head still just as if it were held in place by a steel chain, the wad of thick, hard flesh still down her throat,.

A low moan escapes the man's mouth just as the girl commences an almost silent, desperate whine. The hands guide the girl's head up slowly until his stiff manhood has breached the outside of her lips. She frantically draws a deep breath, her heart pounding with need, her mind dizzy from lack of sustenance. She is allowed one more before the hands push her head forwards once again. She can feel the plush, bulbous head as it glides across the roof of her mouth and over her tongue. She keeps her mouth narrow to maximize the man's pleasure, granting his instrument maximum friction against her moist, hot tissues, and the hard, tubular flesh fills it easily.

Five times the ritualistic fucking of the girl's throat continues. Each time, the man holds her head still a little longer, forcing her to exhaust her reserves of breath. Each time, she breathes deeper when finally released, sucking in air noisily.

The man feels his juices rising and relaxes his grip on the girl's head. This is her signal to begin sucking his cock in earnest, pushing her broad lips along the cock's shaft, circling it with her energetic tongue. Keeping her hands interlocked behind her head, elbows up, she moves rapidly now, drawing a moan from the man each time she pushes her mouth forward, dragging her lips across the hot shaft. He is rocking his hips back and forth in time with the girl's exertions. Suddenly, he gives a loud groan. He barks a command to the woman and begins to pump his hot load of viscous white spume into her mouth. He has ordered her not to swallow and the girl whines as she feels her mouth filling with his spunk. He probes her throat deeply one last time as he growls with pleasure. She can feel it throbbing in her esophagus. When the throbbing slows, he slowly

勢霸

Comfort Girl No. 4

~

Paul Blades

Cover Photo by Canstock Photo, Inc./neotakezu
Copyrite @ Paul Blades 2012
Dark Visions Publicaitons
darkvisionspub@gmail.com

Other Books by Paul Blades:

The Blue Cantina- Books I and II
Klitzman's Isle
Klitzman's empire
Klitzman's Paradise
Klitzman's Pawn- Parts One and Two
Slaver's Dozen- A Tale of Klitzman's Isle
Klitzman's Predators
Three by Blades
The Taking of Cheryl Parts One and Two
Sacrifice to the Emerald God
The Warlord's Concubine, Books 1, 2, 3, & 4
Dreams and Desires, Books One and Two
Carmella Condemned
Carmella's Fate
The Seduction of Morningstar Bridges

The Maddy Saga:

Vol. I	Maddy becomes a Ponygirl
Vol. II	The Training of a Ponygirl
Vol. III	Ponygirl Champion
Vol. IV	Ponygirl Summer
Vol. V	Ponygirl Love
Vol. VI	Ponygirl Season
Vol. VII	Ponygirl Gambit
Vol. VIII	Ponygirl Pleasures
Vol. IX	Ponygirl Peril
Vol. X	Ponygirl's Fate
Vol. XI	Ponygirl's Choice

withdraws it, pushing part of his expenditure out of the girl's mouth and over her lips.

The girl kneels back, and points her dark green eyes at the man expectantly. She has a mouthful of his jism and cannot swallow it or spit it out until she has been given permission. The man looks down at the delightfully formed woman appreciatively. Smiling slightly, as if humored by his own, private joke, he gives her another order and she pulls her hands from behind her head and places them together, palms up, in front of her. Looking up at him as if confirming what he has told her to do, the woman's body shudders in humiliation. She looks down at her hands and squirts the remains of the man's copious discharge on to them. She then raises her hands to her face and covers it with the thick, creamy goo. There is enough to fully cover her face and she has to rub it in so that it does not lay liquid on her skin. Her eyes and mouth are closed as she does so, giving her face a peaceful, contented air that belies her misery and anguish.

When he has satisfied himself that the young girl has complied with his command, the man orders her to resume her former stance. This, like all the previous commands, is given in the harsh, staccato tones of an Asian land. The girl is familiar with them all, having learned their import, if not their meaning, at the end of a whip.

Now, for the first time, the man addresses the woman in English. "Number 7, have you completed the letter?" he demands in a cold, ominous tone. God help her if she hasn't.

The girl takes a deep swallow and responds meekly, her voice barely audible, as if she was out of practice at speaking and was doubtful that the right words would come out. "*Hai, Kanakasama,*" she says, bowing her head.

"Bring it to me," he orders her.

The woman scrambles to the platform in the corner of the room and retrieves the letter, the envelope and the black, felt tip pen. She returns to the feet of her oppressor and hold the materials up to him, her head bent, like an offering to a cruel god.

The man takes the letter and reads it carefully. He grunts his approval and folds it. The girl has kept her arms poised up, the envelope and pen still in her hands. The man places the letter in the envelope and puts it and the pen in his kimono pocket.

"The letter is satisfactory, Number 7. Today you will receive only five lashes," he says matter-of-factly. He pauses, as if contemplating what part of the girl's already marred body will feel the bite of his thin, leather covered reed. She awaits his verdict, shaking in anticipation of the pain of this daily, routine abuse. He utters a command and the girl rapidly turns around and bends over, pushing her hips and her rear high behind her.

Considering his target, the fleshy hindquarters of this desirable young woman, the man rears his right hand back and lets fly. A loud 'crack' permeates the room, followed quickly with the girl's cry of pain. She had clamped her mouth shut, vowing to deprive the man of the satisfaction of the sound of her unhappy suffering, but the pain is so sharp and deep, that she cannot withhold the single, anguished cry. A bright red stripe has formed where the reed has met her flesh and she can feel it burning long after the pain of the impact of the whip subsides. She cries out the word for 'one' in Japanese, "*Ichi!*"

The man takes his time before administering the next blow. Each stroke of the whip is to be savored both by the torturer and the victim. He admires the contrast between the deep, red mark and the girl's pale, white flesh. The girl bemoans her cruel fate as she tries to build up her forces before the next slash of the whip while the burning sting of the last one slowly subsides. Another blow falls. It lands about half an inch above the first. The man is an expert at wielding his instrument and he has carefully measured the blow. "Ahhhhh!" the girl cries out in spite of herself, and then "*Ni!*" as if it was something she had forgotten. "*San!*" she cries out at the third kiss of the cruel whip. "Shi!" and then "*Go!*" Each number is preceded by a screech or yell of pain. Tears are flowing down her face and she is sobbing lowly. She does not understand the cruelty of those who hold her prisoner. She has never experienced anything like it. It holds no place in her perception of the world. But here it is, right behind her, and she can feel the lingering results of this man's cruel bent. The world has changed for her. Silently, in her mind, she begs and pleads to whatever god will listen to change it back.

Having administered the morning's whipping, the man takes time to admire the graceful curves of the posterior presented to him. For a moment he considers ravaging it, as he has done many times before. But the morning is late and he has his rounds to make. "Maybe later," he thinks. Without saying another word to the still supine girl, he turns, unlocks the door and steps out. The unhappy young woman does not move; no one has told her to. She will remain as she is until someone does, bent over on her knees, her forehead to the floor, her red striped, raised rear end proffered to her next visitor.

勢霸

CHAPTER ONE
THE LETTER

Janice Paterson had been living in the city for over two years. She had moved from the distant heartland after college seeking sophistication, adventure, success. She believed she would find it in the fast paced urban core of the country, New York City. After being rejected from every glamorous job she applied for, she had finally taken a job at a mid-sized advertising firm. It was either that or waitressing. When she had come to New York, Janice had looked forward to contact with writers, actors and members of the demi-monde of avant-garde society. Instead, she found herself stuck in a dull and boring job, for the most part a glorified secretary. Her only excitement came from fending off the come-ons from the older, mostly married senior and junior account executives.

She was no schoolgirl, and before coming to the city had permitted a boyfriend or two the ultimate ecstasy of entry into her secret place. But lovemaking for her was not an aerobic event. She treasured the closeness and cuddly feelings and enjoyed the somewhat muted orgasms she had experienced. She performed dutifully what she considered the rather gross task of tonguing and swallowing the ardent tools of her young beaus. She thought it funny, actually, that she could so easily master their desires by a delicate caress on their thighs, a slow, deliberate drawing down of the zipper and a soft murmur in their ear. Once her lips engulfed their swollen members, they were hers to control.

When she arrived in New York, she had initially let go and partied with some of the other young girls in the office. Gradually, however, she gave up the fast life and in the last few months she had only been out on a couple of dates. She had found it hard to make real friends and the men she met were mostly married, gay or losers. She told herself that she could live without men and sex for the time being as she worked hard to learn as much as she could about the advertising business. An occasional self-administered caress was enough to keep her sexual urges on the back burner. She permitted herself these little twirky orgasms, as weak as a kitten's sneeze and almost as quick, on a weekly basis, often on a Saturday night, usually after watching a tear jerking romance on DVD.

This Tuesday evening had begun like over a hundred Tuesdays before with her release from work and a short subway ride uptown to her small three-room apartment. She picked up her mail, as usual, and as she ascended the four flights of stairs to her lodgings, rifled through it absent-mindedly. She could have used the elevator; the building had a dingy passenger elevator in the front foyer and a larger, dingier freight elevator in the back. But Janice preferred the stairs. She was trim, had been an athlete in college. A member of the freshman and sophomore track teams, she had continued a regimen of fitness even after she decided that she needed more time to devote to her studies and gave up organized sports. Team sports such as softball and soccer did not appeal to her. She loved swimming, but her voluptuous body was not built for competitive swimming. And her hair. Long, brown with a reddish streak, she could not have sacrificed it to the demands of speed in the swimming pool.

So she walked the stairs, slowly but steadily, thumbing through the mail as she rose up the steps. Bills, circulars, a letter from her friend Denise and a sort of funny brown envelope marked "Open Immediately" in big red letters. As she entered her tiny apartment, she tossed the circulars in the circular file, placed the bills on the small table by the door and put Denise's letter in her pocket. This she would read in her bath. She was about to toss the brown envelope with the demanding instruction in the waste can when she hesitated. "Mmmmm", she thought, "maybe I'll check this out later. I'll find out what's so damn important in the world of junk mail." Taking a step or two into the apartment, she thought again, "Nah, who needs more insurance, credit cards, collectables or whatever they're selling anyhow." She turned and tossed the envelope into the can.

Janice quickly microwaved a hot cup of Orange Pekoe tea and proceeded to run her bath, being careful to add in a few measured drops of body oil. She loved to make her skin soft and smooth, and the oil and hot water seemed to relax her just right. She stripped off the summer dress and placed the letter and her tea on the chair next to the tub. Tossing aside her dainty under things, she stepped in the tub slowly, but deliberately. As she eased her body down, she uttered a soft sigh, not unlike the sigh exuded during the sexual act when her lower place was finally entered by a sturdy male member, soft and slow, as she liked it.

Having braved the steaming, slightly stinging heat of the water, she relaxed. After a minute or two of almost stupefied languor, she stretched out her arm absent mindedly to retrieve her cup of tea. Slowly sipping the steaming brew, her decompression was complete. She put the tea down and leaned back, prepared to drift lazily into a trance like state. Her hands lay lightly on her lean stomach, rubbing gently in a slow, circular motion. The hot oily water made her skin soft and tingly. Inevitably, her hands fell lower, pulled down by their own weight. Finally, they found what her mind had unconsciously sought, the center of her desire.

At first, her hands gently stroked the inside of her thighs, her fingers running lightly over the sides of her generous mons. "Mmmm," she thought, "its not Saturday, but it feels so good." As of their own volition, her fingers found her pouting lips. Gently pushing them apart, her right hand found its customary place, stroking the narrow slit between. Her left sought a more specific spot, the tiny button above.

She took her time, feeling the warmth of her rising lust spread throughout her body. From time to time, one hand or the other would leave its loving task, to rise and caress her now passion engorged nipples. Panting, she could feel the juices rise within her. Frightened of her own sexual urgency, she backed off, slowing her approach to the mountaintop. No earth moving orgasms for her. Control, that was her polestar.

When she could wait no longer, she allowed the pressure to build. Her heart started to pounding in her chest, her breasts seemed likely to burst, her hands, busily drawing her closer and closer to her goal. When the tide seemed poised to overwhelm her, she tightened her legs around her hands, clutching her sex, holding the passion in. Her whole body tensed as she steeled her muscles against the threatened onslaught. Her back arched, her face pulled tight into a grimace. Finally, she climaxed, her body twitching in resistance, reducing what could have been to a few small impulses of pleasure.

When the spasms subsided, she slowly relaxed. "Whew," she thought, "that was nice." She had almost given in, but her will had overborne her physical sensations. The result was as if she had been through a wrestling match with herself; tired, at ease, yet physically somehow not quite satisfied.

Janice let herself drift a while, letting the warm water finish the job that her self ministrations had begun. When she felt finally fully physically at peace, she opened her eyes. The room was somehow friendlier, the hazy steam settling about her like a warm blanket. She remembered her tea and reached out and took a generous gulp. Placing the cup back on the chair, she spied the letter from Denise.

After carefully drying her hands on the towel draped across the nearby chair, Janice picked up the letter. Funny, she thought, she had not been able to get Denise on the phone for several weeks. Normally, they spoke once or twice a week, girl talk, mostly, a great way of letting off the tensions of being a poor girl in the city. Of course, Denise was in a different city, clear across the continent.

They had both fled the stifling confines of their small Ohio town, but in different directions. Denise to L.A., Janice to New York. But they had both sought the same things: bright lights, big city.

Denise was the more "artsy-fartsy" of the two and longed for the golden screen. She had gotten a job in a talent agency, entry level of course, and had learned a hundred ways to make coffee. She had told Janice of her "relationships" with the stars, and would-be stars, all of whom shared a common quality. They all were assholes. The men, when they deigned to speak to her at all, had that tell-tale, 'wouldn't you like to fuck me?' look in their eyes. The women barely even saw Denise, looked right through her, as if she were some kind of handmaiden.

Janice and Denise had shared the details of their love life too. In spite of her disdain for the self-absorbed, conceited pretty boys who came through the office seeking stardom, Denise had found a few attractive enough to see what they could do for her between the sheets. It was mostly disappointing, but one or two had rung her bell. They were not keepers, however, and Denise had been happy enough when their attentions focused back on themselves or to the job of fucking someone who could actually help their careers. Denise had even succumbed to the seductions of one of the lady would-be's, something that had initially shocked Janice, but not enough to stop her from drawing out every little detail from her friend. The affair had been as short lived as all the others, especially as Denise had discovered that a plastic "Steely Dan" could not compare to the hot, throbbing real thing. On the other hand, the lady did give good head.

So Janice was happy to finally get some news from Denise. Janice had called Denise's agency a couple of times, only to be told that Denise was "on assignment", "on vacation" or "out". Denise had phoned back, but only to leave vague, terse messages on Janice's machine. The last one had been about two weeks ago and Janice was beginning to think that the continent which separated them was going to prove too far a distance to sustain their friendship. But now, a letter. Cool.

Janice carefully tore open the side of the envelope and let Denise's letter slip out. Not what she would call a missive. A single one sided sheet of writing. Janice suppressed her disappointment and read the graceful cursive script which was Denise's typical handiwork:

Janice,

I'm sorry I have not been able to speak to you in the last couple of months. I have been very busy and tied up in a new project. I can't tell you much about it only that it has taken up all my attention. My new employers are looking for more single women like you and me to fill out their requirements. It's an unusual opportunity for you to see a whole new side of life. If you are interested, you should respond to the circular they will be sending you. It will probably come in the mail the same day as this letter. If you call the number in the circular, you can be sure that all of your financial problems will be in the past.

I have to go now but I'm sure we'll have some contact in the near future.

Love, Denise.

P.S. Don't forget to act right away!

Janice was puzzled by the terse letter Denise had written. While Denise was not a prolific writer, the few letters she had sent had been filled with the minutiae of her life, more like a stream of consciousness picture of her heart. The letters had been warm and funny, but this one was like a business letter, cold and empty of real content. It almost seemed like a form letter. And Denise never ended her letters "Love, Denise". All of her letters had ended with an endearing inscription, "Your best friend" or "Your partner in adventure" or something like that.

Well, although they had talked many times over the last two years, they were many miles apart and maybe they were both going through changes that would eventually leave their friendship behind. Apparently this new job or whatever it was had taken all of Denise's free time. She had always been one to throw herself into new things.

Janice placed the letter aside and completed her ablutions in the bath. After drying herself, rubbing some of that deliciously smelling powder on her intimates, and a long session with the dryer on her hair, she was ready for some dinner. She donned a silky robe and went to the kitchenette off of the small dining room. The apartment was typically small, as New York rents were atrocious. But she loved the view from her living area and the unusually large bedroom. And, oh, closets, there were closets.

After broiling her small filet of skinless chicken (no frying for the weight conscious), steaming a small piece of broccoli and boiling a smattering of whole wheat noodles, Janice sat at the small dining room table and flipped on the television. The news was boring, the talk shows were boring and the movies were boring. Well, it was just background noise anyway. She remembered then the envelope she had tossed in the waste can. "Open Immediately!" Janice wondered if that was the envelope that Denise had talked about in her letter. Well, if she wanted to more about more know what Denise was up to she should read it.

Janice retrieved the oversized brown envelope from the hallway trashcan and returned to her dinner. She opened the envelope and read its contents as she carefully masticated her "diet delight".

Inside was a single 8 ½ x 11" page of glossy paper, oversized to match the envelope. Across the top in a banner headline was the words "ONCE IN A LIFETIME....." There was a picture of a trio of happy women holding hands and marching towards the viewer. All of the women were beautiful, had long, flowing hair, and were wearing short, clinging, colorful dresses that showed off their long and tanned legs.

Underneath the picture, again in banner headlines "FINANCIAL SECURITY CAN BE YOURS!" Janice read the blue colored text that ran below the banner:

> "Yes, lifetime financial security can be yours! An international company is seeking talented and vibrant young women to act as representatives in worldwide trade. Lifetime financial security guaranteed. Our client demands the most loyal and personable employees to assist in the marketing of its worldwide products and services. Significant training provided at our modern facilities. Call today."

The advertisement went on for a few more paragraphs touting the benefits of financial security and lamenting the need for absolute confidentiality. No substance though. Not even a name of the company. Just an "800" number to call "day or night".

Janice pondered the ad and wondered what the hell this could be all about. It was hard to believe that it was a legitimate offer. She was all too aware of the implications of things too good to be true. Nothing was as simple as this ad suggested. And oddly, there didn't seem to be any company name in the ad. But then again, if Denise was doing it, and had written to her about it, wasn't it worth a little phone call? The ad stated that, "All calls are strictly confidential." And, "All it takes is one phone call." Well, maybe tomorrow.

The next day was a more than typical day at the office for Janice. The telephone was ringing off of the hook, her boss, that asshole, yelled at her for screwing up an appointment and it rained all day. When she got home to her apartment she was beat and depressed. More bills in the mail, more ads. She hesitated before taking her normal four-story trek. The weight of the day seemed to bore down on her and she decided to forgo her regimen this day. Tomorrow, she'd do the stairs, but just this once, she needed to rest and recuperate from the day's depressing events.

Janice walked off of the elevator and lunged into her apartment. This was her sanctuary, her walls like the battlements of a castle. She could recuperate here.

Again, somewhat out of character, Janice decided to have a small glass of wine before her bath. Better than tea, she thought. She pulled the cork from a bottle of Merlot she had been saving for a special event and poured herself a nice glassful. Walking the short distance to her small living area, she plopped herself down on the sofa/futon she had bought many months ago to serve the dual purpose as furniture and a guest bed. After taking a long drink from the delicate stemware, she sat back and just sighed. "This fucking job is going nowhere fast," she thought. "One more day like this and I'll open one of these windows and leap out."

Janice picked up the remote and clicked on the stereo. A nice soothing CD, the mystical notes of Emmett Charles on the sax, wafted out to her. "Mmmm," she thought, "that's more like it." She put down the glass and reached behind her, lifting her hips. Grabbing the elastic waistband of her pantyhose, she pulled it down over her hips and then down her long, well trimmed legs. She hated pantyhose, but garter belts and such were such a pain. And the nylons did accentuate the shapeliness of her legs well. "What self respecting girl would go out without good stockings," she thought.

She tossed the pantyhose aside and reached for another pull on the wine. She was beginning to feel human again. She closed her eyes and drifted as the music washed over her. Those high saxophone notes seemed to pierce her. She was beginning to feel that warm and fuzzy feeling. Rubbing her hands over her thighs, and between them, she looked forward to her bath. "Two days in a row? Well why not", she thought.

After about twenty minutes, long enough for several cuts off of Emmett Charles's latest, and long enough to finish off the Merlot in her glass, Janice arose from the couch. She was slightly tipsy from three glasses of wine, and edgy from horniness, the result of an absentminded, but steady, caress of her sex. The combination of a wine buzz and a sex buzz made her laconic, but with a heightened awareness.

Janice walked by the dining room table and retrieved the Merlot bottle for recorking. As she did, she spotted the circular from the day before. It lay half hidden on the table, covered with today's disappointing mail. Janice picked it up. Looking again at the smiling face of the models on the brochure she said to herself, "Well, why the fuck not?"

After a day like today, Janice was willing to grasp at straws. Maybe a new opportunity is just what she needed. She was going nowhere fast at Grayson's Advertising. Her boss, Mr. Jennings was a pain in the ass, always coming on to her. He had piled tons of work on her, even forcing her to sign and submit his expense vouchers. He did all the traveling and each time he returned Janice had to trot down to bookkeeping, turn in his voucher and bring the $300 or $400 dollars in expense cash back to him. Why the company still dealt in cash was a wonder to her, but it was a symptom of its backwardness. Enough was enough.

Summoning up her courage, Janice dialed the 800 number on the cover of the brochure. Janice didn't like speaking to strangers, especially on the phone. She felt a little bit better about calling since she thought that she would probably get a recording instructing her to call during business hours. She was surprised when she heard an operator's voice answer the third ring with "Enterprises".

The voice was almost mechanical, possibly even a recording. This was not a good start. Janice almost returned the telephone to its cradle. She looked at the happy women on the brochure and determined to proceed. "Hello, I'm calling about the circular on the employment opportunity..." Janice didn't really know how else to describe it.

The voice seemed to respond to her question, "Please state the name of the person who referred you".

Janice felt funny about giving information to what seemed to be a machine. Well, Denise <u>had</u> written about the job and they obviously already knew about her since she worked there. Janise answered, "Denise Thrombly".

The machine responded "Please hold".

There was a whirring sound in the phone and several clicks. This time a male voice answered. A male voice with a slight accent, perhaps Japanese or Chinese. Anyway, this voice was live. "Is this Ms. Janice Paterson?"

Janice was somewhat taken aback. But then again, if it was an efficient company, they would have a record of who had been referred by Denise. They would even probably have caller i.d. Well, so much for privacy. Janice hesitatingly said, "Yes".

The male voice continued. "Do you desire to apply for a position?"

Janice again, surprised at the directness of the question, hesitated. Did she want to apply? Well, she had called, hadn't she? But.... Janice spoke softly into the telephone, "Well, I read your brochure and I..."

"Please Ms. Paterson, I need to know whether you wish to apply for a position with our organization."

Janice replied, "I don't know, what jobs are available?"

"Please, Ms. Paterson, all that information will be made available to you. What I need to know is do you wish to apply for a position?"

Janice let a few moments pass. There was silence on the line. She reviewed briefly in her mind the consequences of saying yes. If they searched her references it might get back to her boss and she could be fired. Well, who gave a shit about that? There were plenty of dead end jobs in this town. And she could always turn down anything that was offered to her, couldn't she?

"Y-yes, o.k., yes, I'd like to apply." Janice said hesitatingly.

The voice quickly responded. "Your application is accepted. Please review the notice that will be sent to you for receipt tomorrow. Please comply with its instructions."

"No, no, you don't understand...I...," Janice stammered into the phone. But the voice had already disconnected.

"Well, that was weird," Janice thought. The voice said that her application was accepted. Did that mean that they were acknowledging her application and would get back to her or did it mean that she was accepted into the job? But how could either be true if she didn't give the voice any information?

"Anyway," she thought, "who would want to work for a strange organization like that?" And it made her creepy that they knew her name as soon as she called. Another one of those offers too good to be true.

The next day, Janice followed her daily routine without deviation. Off to work, back to home. As she brought in the mail, she noticed a small envelope addressed to her with a New York postmark. Holding the envelope up to the light, she saw that it contained a small card. Janice pretty much knew what it was. It was that awful job thing. She tossed the envelope into the garbage.

In the morning, Janice was just leaving her apartment building to walk to the subway stop two blocks away when she saw a limousine parked just opposite her doorway. A slight, Asian gentleman was standing there. He wore a limo driver's getup, cap and all. He seemed to recognize her as she stepped onto the sidewalk.

"Missy, I am driver, please get in car," the man said politely.

Janice stopped and looked at him strangely. Then it hit her, this was from that odd company. The envelope last night probably told her that someone would be by to pick her up. She really should have called them and told them to forget it, but who would have expected this?

"Ah, no thanks" Janice told the driver. "I'm not going, but thanks anyway."

The driver seemed disturbed by Janice's statement. He stepped forward to her. Janice noticed that the man's slight build hid a well-muscled and well toned body. The man moved like a cat. He got just a little too close for Janice's comfort. "You must come. You have been accepted. I am to take you for your training."

Janice stood back a step. "Training?" she thought, "What training?" She stepped back again, more nervous now. "N-no thanks, I said." Janice blurted out. "Please leave me alone."

The man looked around at the heavy pedestrian traffic and then back at Janice. He shrugged his shoulders and turned to walk back to the limo. Janice, relieved that he had backed off, quickly stepped away.

Later that afternoon, as she was sitting at her desk, opening the afternoon inter-office mail, the telephone rang. Janice could tell from the ring that it was an outside call, direct to her line. Not too many people had that number so she figured it was probably a friend or something important.

"Hello, Janice Paterson speaking."

"Ms. Paterson, you missed your appointment today. We are very displeased with you."

It was the voice from the phone, from the weird company. How did they get her work number? They were going to get her fired! Well, she would put an end to this right away.

"Listen, I never said I would take a job from your company. I don't like the way you do business. I'm sorry but I am not taking a job from you. So please leave me alone and don't call on this line again."

Janice hung up the telephone. That should put an end to that, she thought. Again, she didn't like the menace in the voice, different from the voice's tone the night before, but much alike to the driver from this morning. Well, it was all over now, anyway.

When she came home that night, Janice found a note slipped under her door. It was a small card, smaller than an index card, white, with simple writing. It was addressed to her. It said simply:

> To: Janice Paterson
> Re: Job Training
>
> Please present yourself to the company's driver tomorrow at 8:15 A.M. for transportation to commencement of your training program.

Janice was startled. Was this card from the night before or did these people really not get it? Well, if they didn't get her message, she would file a harassment charge against them.

As Janice made her dinner, took her bath and relaxed in front of her TV, she stewed about the card and the phone call of that afternoon. She was just about ready to turn in when the telephone rang. Janice checked the call waiting and saw that the number was blocked. She had a good idea who it was. It was probably the stupid company. Well, she wasn't going to answer it.

After the fifth ring, Janice's answering machine kicked in. After her cute little message, a voice came on the line. It was the same guy.

"Ms. Paterson, I know that you are home and that you are listening to this. You have been instructed to present yourself for training for your new position with our company. Failure to make the appointment will disappoint us greatly. Goodbye."

Janice shook her head. These people just didn't give up. If that car was there again the next morning she would notify the police. Enough was enough!

Just as promised, the limo was there the next morning n front of Janice's building. The little Asian guy was there too. He stood by the limo with the door opened invitingly. Janice ignored his gesture and walked away as fast as she could.

At lunchtime, she called the local precinct. She was referred to the citizen complaint department and told her story to a somewhat incredulous police officer. He assured her that these people would give up and he didn't see anything threatening or menacing in what Janice had told him. "Just walk away ma'm. You should be honored that they want you that badly."

Janice slammed the telephone down in disgust. "What an asshole!" she thought. "I can't believe these people can keep hassling me and get away with it." Well, if all she could do was ignore them then that's what she would do.

That night, Janice treated herself to an extra orgasm as she lay in her tub. She was well relaxed when she prepared for bed. She wore nothing but her panties and a t-shirt when she slept. She climbed in, turned off the light and pulled up the covers. There had been no telephone call that night. Maybe the cop was right. Maybe they would just go away.

In the middle of the night, Janice woke up with a start. Her heart jumped into her throat as she felt a hand across her mouth and the pressure of a massive body leaning over her. The room was lit only by the glow from the streetlamps outside. As she started to struggle, she felt another hand grab her around the throat and squeeze.

Well, that was the end of the struggle to get free; now she was struggling for air. She felt legs wrap around hers, her arms pinned to her body by the arms of her assailant. As the need for air began to get acute, Janice felt an odd detachment. She was angry at herself to let herself get murdered in her own apartment. She could hear her mother's "I told you so's", even though she knew that, if she was dead, she would not get the chance to hear her mother's reprobation.

Just as her consciousness was beginning to wane, Janice felt the hand around her neck ease up. She gasped for air through her nose as her mouth was still encumbered by the man's other hand. She made a slight whinnying noise as she tried to draw as much air into her lungs as she could. Then the man holding her spoke.

The voice was deep, with a strong accent, almost certainly Asian. The words were spoken softly but sternly. "Make no talk. Make noise and be hurt, understand?"

Janice shook her head affirmatively as decisively as she could, given the hand over her mouth and the huge body crushing her. The hand pulled back from her mouth, letting her draw breath, but keeping pressure on her cheeks. Janice knew that if she made the slightest sound, the hand would be back and then she would be in for it. Maybe this guy wouldn't hurt her if she cooperated? That's what they said, didn't they, cooperate and live or fight and die. If she was going to be raped, there was nothing she could do about it now.

Finally, the man's hand left her face. She remained pinned to the bed on her back, the man's legs athwart her body, locking her legs into place. Janice felt the man reaching for something and then heard a ripping noise, as if he had ripped the bed sheet. In a second, she discovered what had caused the noise as the man pressed a wide piece of duct tape across her mouth.

"Oh, god, not gagged!" Janice thought. As the tape was pressed home, she, for the first time, began to panic. This was becoming all too real.

The man then lifted his weight off of Janice's body and pushed her over onto her stomach. He held her hands together behind her back in a vice-like grip. His hands were big, able to encompass both her wrists. She felt the man fumbling and then heard the ripping sound again. He was going to tie her hands, Janice realized. "He's going to tie me up and do things to me. Oh, god, please help me!"

Janice was right. The man circled her wrists with the tape, first across and then over and under her wrists. He did this twice and then tore off the end.

Janice's hands were now tightly tied behind her back. For a moment, the man sat his huge bulk on the backs of Janice's legs. Janice could feel a hardness pressing against the lower portion of her rear end. It could only be one thing, and it was. The man had obviously enjoyed the act of subduing her. Janice knew it and, in her panic, imagined what would come next. She was wrong.

Sliding himself down towards the foot of the bed, the man quickly wrapped Janice's ankles with tape, locking them together. He then pulled Janice's body so that her feet now rested on the floor and her torso on the bed. More tape around Janice's thighs. Each time the man used the tape, Janice could hear the ripping sound, a terrifying sound to her in her predicament. As if something was being torn apart.

The man's next move, he worked silently, was to pull Janice's panties down off of her hips, under her belly and down to where the tape around her thighs began. Janice tried to struggle as her white, tender backside was exposed to view. Even in the dim light from the street, her baby soft ass almost glinted. For the first time since her ordeal began, Janice began to cry. Not hysterically, but mournfully, silently. She could feel the tears running slowly down her face. She tried to stop, tried to marshal her dignity and inner strength, but this effort was interrupted by the next development in her predicament.

Since she was distracted, Janice did not hear the slithering sound of a leather belt being removed from the belt loops of the man's trousers. She did not see the man wind the belt around his hand so that it was short enough to swing accurately at a close target. She did feel the man's hand press against her back, forcing her down, pinning her to the mattress. Janice did hear the swish of the belt's whip end now rushing through the air, but it occurred too close in time to her next sensation to be remarked.

'Crack!' The belt was laid across the alabaster skin of Janice's ass. Janice's body stiffened as if electrified. She was about to cry out when another blow landed. 'Crack!'

The pain was exquisite; a burning, stinging pain. Another blow landed and Janice began to scream behind her duct taped lips. Only a high pitched, muffled screech emerged. Janice tried to get up, move away from the force of the blows, but the man's hand, pressed into the center of her back, held her down. 'Crack!' Another blow struck her, this time across the bottom part of her ass, the underside, where her ass met her thighs. This blow landed dangerously close to Janice's treasure, and she almost gagged at the thought of being whipped there.

'Crack!' This time the blow landed across her thighs, not as pale as her rear, but tender all the same. Janice was now balling uncontrollably behind her gag. The unreality of being whipped in her own bedroom by this strong, silent assailant was negated by the excruciating, very real pain Janice was receiving.

Janice tried to move her feet, but the man had trapped them with his own. She could do nothing to prevent the man's presumed pleasure at administering this almost juvenile beating. 'Crack! Crack! Crack!' the belt came down sharply against her thighs. And then the backs of her lower legs, three blows across them. The man then paused. Janice was still sobbing uncontrollably. As if he had decided that he had made his point, whatever that was, he released his hand from Janice's back and allowed her to free her legs from his. Janice almost slid off of the bed having gone virtually limp with shock and pain. The man prevented her from sliding off and actually pulled her back up so that her entire body was now fully on the bed, her head now resting on her pillows.

Janice sobbed, sobbing as if the whole world had betrayed her. Her whole safe, comfortable world was dissolved by this man's violent assault against her in her own bedroom, an assault that she was powerless to prevent or ameliorate.

Suddenly, Janice felt the man's hand reach once more around her throat. He pulled her head back, causing Janice to gurgle and moan. "Was he going to strangle her now?"

Janice thought in headlong panic. "Oh no, no, no, please, God, I want to live!"

But the man had no intention of strangling Janice, for she was not merely an object for the man's pleasure, although he did enjoy his work. No, Janice was an employee of the company that had sent him here. She was a disobedient employee and had earned this punishment.

As Janice ceased blubbering behind her gag, the man forced her to look directly into his face. It was the first time she had gotten a chance to take a good look at him. His face was broad, his eyes, slits; a scar ran down his left cheek. His nose was deformed like a prizefighter's. It was a face Janice would never forget, a cold, mean visage. Certain that he had Janice's attention, the man spoke for the second time that night.

"Bad girl, naughty girl. You take limo tomorrow. No fool around."

Janice's head began to whirl. She had not connected the disembodied phone messages or the tiny, almost comical man who had stood by the limousine for the past two mornings with this invasion of her home, with her torture by this hulk of a man. But like lightening, she understood. And her blood ran cold.

The man left Janice still tied on her bed. When she heard her apartment door close, she began to struggle to liberate herself. It took the best part of an hour, but she was finally able to get her hands free. After she had removed the tape from the rest of her body, she crawled into a ball on her bed and cried.

As she lay there, she began to try and understand the evening's events. "What is going on?" she thought to herself. She could not understand how one telephone call had resulted in this hellish predicament. This man had entered her apartment like he had a key. If it were not for the tangled, used tape lying on the floor and the still sore remnants of her whipping, Janice could almost believe that this had been a nightmare. But it wasn't a nightmare, it was real. The mangled tape she had removed from her body was there on the floor. Her legs and bottom still burned from her beating. What was she going to do?

Janice did not remember when she got back to sleep. She awoke in a cold sweat, a terrible dream still in her mind. She was being chased, by whom she did not know. Every time that she thought she had gotten ahead of her pursuers, she would end up at the beginning where they were standing, waiting for her. In the dream it seemed that she repeated this cycle a dozen times. The disconcerting nature of the dream added to Janice's anxiety about what to do next. She certainly was not getting in the limo! Her only alternative was to call the police.

She spoke to a dispatcher, after calling 911. She waited two hours before detectives arrived. There were two of them. One was an older, balding guy, with wire rim glasses and grey hair. He wore a wrinkled grey suit and a narrow black tie. He did most of the questioning. The other detective was young, maybe 25 or 26 years old. He was a sharp dresser and wore a well tailored, blue, pin striped suit and a paisley tie. His hair was jet black and cut close to his head. His face was friendly, but his manner was diffident. He spent most of the time walking around the apartment, looking at things.

The grey haired detective wanted to know how the intruder had 'gained admittance'. Janice couldn't tell him.

"Well, ma'm, we've looked at the locks and they haven't been jimmied. The windows all look all right. You sure you didn't give your key to nobody?"

Janice was incensed at the implication. "Do you think that I go around giving out my key to strangers?" she asked, huffily. "No one has my key except the super."

"Well, this guy must be awfully good if he can beat a double lock on the door without leaving a mark."

"I don't know about that officer…." Janice began.

"Detective, ma'm."

"Yes, Detective. Anyway I don't know how he got in, but he did. Do you think that I tied myself up? That I beat myself?"

"No, I don't ma'm, but I have to go on evidence. I have seen the duct tape on the floor, but I haven't seen anything else that corroborates your story."

"God damn it!" Janice began.

"Hold on, lady. I didn't say we wouldn't investigate. What you're alleging is a very serious thing. We're gonna have a fingerprint team here later and they'll go over everything. With your permission, we'll look at telephone records. And we'll keep a blue and white parked outside for a couple of days in case the limo shows up again."

"You mean that you didn't see it?" Janice cried. "It's been there all morning. Just look out the window!"

Janice's living room window gave a good view of the street by the entrance to her building. She led the detective to it and looked down. The limo was not there.

"I don't see a limo, ma'm, do you?" the detective asked neutrally.

"No…I don't," Janice replied, mystified. But then they probably saw the cops pull up. "Did you drive up in a police car, detective?" she asked.

"No ma'm, an unmarked car."

"But they might have seen you, right?"

"Ma'm, some people say they can smell a cop when one walks in the door. We just try and look like everybody else. I don't know if we spooked them, but if they're back tomorrow, we'll question them."

"Question them?" Janice asked, incredulous. "You mean you won't arrest them?"

"Ms. Paterson," the detective answered, "we don't have any real evidence that connects the guy who was in your apartment, if there was a guy, with the limo guy. We'll need more than some duct tape on the floor."

Janice was mad. She had suffered a considerable amount of pain and great indignity. She didn't know whether she could spend another night in the apartment. And these guys were acting as if she had made the whole thing up! "Detective Grey…," Janice started to shout.

"That's Guray, ma'm, Detective Guray."

"Okay, Detective Guray, what about the fact that I was beaten?" Janice asked.

"We only have your word for that Ms. Paterson. There's no sign of any disturbance in the apartment, no sign of forced entry. And you deny that anyone else had a key but you and the super. What can I say?"

All this time, the junior detective had been snooping around the apartment. He took note of the books on Janice's bookshelf, the breakfast dishes, what was in the dishwasher, the garbage. He hadn't said a word until now.

"Miss," he said, "if we had pictures of the injuries, that would at least be something."

"Pictures?" Janice queried in a high, indignant screech. "Pictures of my ass?"

"To put it in a single word, miss, yes. If that's where you say the injuries occurred."

"Okay," Janice said. If that's what it will take, but I want a female photographer."

Det. Guray reasserted his authority. "Ma'm," he said, "we don't have a female photographer in our precinct. They may have some downtown or in other precincts. But getting them could take some time, probably days. The marks, if there are marks, would be gone by then. If you are willing to have pictures taken so that we can document your injuries, it will have to be now. I don't think the Captain is going to send a photographer up here today. We've got three homicides from last night to investigate."

"Y,you mean that you would take the pictures yourselves," Janice stuttered.

"Yes, ma'm, we have a camera. A digital camera. If you want, we could take the pictures."

"I don't know…." Janice started to answer.

"That's okay," Guray stated. "Let's go, Don." He said to the other detective. To Janice he said, "Here's my card, ma'm. If anything comes up, we'll let you know."

Janice took the card and watched as the detective started to walk away. "Wait! Stop!" Janice called. The detective turned around.

"I'll let you do it, but just you."

"Ma'm," Det. Guray advised Janice, "you don't understand evidence rules. If I take the pictures, I need someone to testify that they saw me take them. And it can't be you. It should be another police officer. Now Detective Grower is an experienced police officer and detective. We've both seen lots of things. We're sensitive to your feelings. But if he doesn't watch while I take the shots, they're worthless."

Janice stood there and took all of this in. It didn't make any sense to her, but then she wasn't a police officer. To have that gorgeous looking cop staring at her naked ass was almost too much. But if she needed the pictures to get help from the police, she should do it.

"Okay," she said at last.

"That's good, ma'm. Let's go into the bedroom and we can try and reenact it, okay?"

"Okay," Janice murmured.

The trio went back into the bedroom. Janice hesitated. She had donned clean panties and a pair of slacks this morning before she called 911 and then her office to let them know she would be late. She wore a short sleeved, poplin blouse. He breasts peaked nicely.

"You'll have to get on the bed, ma'm and show us how you were laying. Then you can pull down your slacks and panties and show us your a…, I mean marks," the detective stated.

Janice caught the "ass" remark. Maybe she should forget this, she thought. But Janice thought again of the giant Asian man and the limo downstairs. She needed the help of the police. She would have to do it.

Janice leaned her long, thin torso over the bed. Her rear was thrust slightly in the air and her legs were pressed against the end of the mattress. "Here's how I was when he whipped me," she said. She could hear the camera clicking as she spoke.

"Okay, ma'm, I got those shots, now I need you to pull down your pants."

Janice hesitated, but then reached around her front and undid the snap to her slacks. She had to stand to wriggle them down; they were kind of tight. She faced away from the officers, not wanting to see them watching her. She also didn't want her face in any of the pictures, in case they showed up on the internet or something.

When she finally got her pants and panties to her ankles, she leaned over the bed once more. The evidence of her thrashing was still there, although somewhat faded. Janice heard the telltale clicking of the camera.

She was so embarrassed! She kept her legs locked together as tight as she could, but she knew that a tiny bit of pubic hair and even the outline of her pussy's slit could probably be seen. In fact, it could be seen jammed between her compressed thighs. Don elbowed Guray to get a good shot of it. It seemed to Janice that they were taking a lot of pictures of her ass.

"Ma'm, I need you to turn your head so that we can get a picture of your face," Guray told her.

"No way," Janice exclaimed. Her head was down. It was weird talking to someone you couldn't see, especially when you were bare assed in your own bedroom. "No way am I going to let you put my face in any of those pictures!" she said. "I don't know who's going to see them. No way."

"Ms. Paterson," Guray started again, "I'm sorry, but we need a picture of your face. If we don't, then, if you'll pardon me, ma'm, this could be anybody's um, eh…posterior," the detective said, obviously searching for the most polite way of saying 'ass'. "If we don't get the head shot," he continued, "these pictures might be ruled out of evidence by a judge. Then you would have gone through this for nothing."

A silence ensued. Janice was highly conscious of her exposed ass while she gave the issue some thought. She could hear the rustling of clothing and the shifting of the detectives' feet behind her. Once she heard some whispering between the men and thought she heard a suppressed snicker.

"God damn it!" she thought. "Okay," she said, "but just one."

"We'll need at least three, ma'm, in case the others don't come out."

"All right, three!" Janice replied, exasperated.

"Okay, ma'm, please turn your head."

Janice turned her head to look back at the detectives. Det. Guray held the camera and was taking shots of her face and ass. He stood back a couple of feet to get both in the shot. The other detective was standing there, a Mona Lisa smile on his face.

"Shit!" Janice thought. "This is fucking ridiculous!" She stood up and began to pull up her panties and slacks. She had to jiggle her hips to get the pants all the way to her waist. She was conscious of a little roll of fat on her hips and the detectives' staring eyes. When she was fully dressed again, she turned and said to the detectives, "Okay, then, that's it."

"That's all we need, ma'm," Det. Guray stated. "Thank you." Janice showed the detectives out. As they were going down the elevator, they both broke out into hearty laughs.

勢霸

CHAPTER TWO
FLIGHT

Janice went to work after the detectives left. She told the super to admit the fingerprint people when they came. She was sitting by her computer at the office when she received a notice that she had new email. She went to her server and saw an email with a reference of "Police Investigation". She opened it.

The email read as follows:

"Dear Ms. Paterson:

> It is unfortunate that you have involved the police department in our personal business relationship. You also failed to meet your obligation to report to our offices for new employee orientation and training. Please be advised that we take our relationship as employer/employee very seriously. If you do not fulfill your obligations, we will have to consider more serious steps to insure performance of your responsibilities."

The message was unsigned. The email address that it had come from was <u>enterprises@opportunity.com</u>. An innocuous, probably untraceable address.

Janice was flabbergasted. She had spoken to the police no more than two hours ago. How could they know that? And how did they get her email address? There was a jpg file attached to the message. Reluctantly, she clicked on it and opened it. It was a picture of her leaning over her bed, her pants around her ankles. She was peering back at the camera. It was one of the pictures the detectives had taken that morning!

Janice panicked. These people seemed to know everything about her. Even her reports to the police were not safe. How could she sleep in her apartment? How could she remain in New York? She was probably being watched right now!

Janice stood up and looked around the office. Her desk was in the middle of a large group of offices, cubbyholes really. There was Marie and Jimmy talking at the cooler. Bob was leaning over Marsha's divider, leering at her. Janice did not see anyone watching her.

Nonetheless, she was not comforted. A shivering cold went down her spine. Who were these people and how powerful were they? Janice decided that she couldn't take a chance. She decided that she would drive to Ohio and move in with her folks for a few weeks. It was three o'clock. If she left right now, she could be almost out of Jersey before 5. She would stay overnight somewhere in central Pennsylvania and drive the rest of the way in the morning. She would call work in the morning and give a family emergency as her excuse.

But she needed clothes, a toothbrush, other toiletries. She dared not go to her apartment. If she did, these people would be sure to stop her. Then she remembered that her exercise bag was at the gym. She had clean underwear and toiletries in there. She could swing by and pick it up. It was only three blocks from the office.

She also needed to rent a car. She would do that over the Internet at her health club. Janice stood up, grabbed her pocketbook and walked calmly to the elevator. She felt that someone was staring at her back all the way. She waited patiently for the elevator door to open and stepped in. When she turned around, she saw nothing.

Forty five minutes later, Janice was on Route 80 heading west. It was about 5:30 and traffic had jammed up a bit. But she knew that she would make eastern PA in about an hour and a half. She would drive for another hour and then find a motel and proceed in the morning.

It was actually closer to 11 P.M. that Janice pulled into a strip motel just on the other side of exit 247. It was straight out of central casting. The sign said 'MOT L', and that there were '...acancies'. The motel office was a square of glass with a small room in the back. The guy behind the counter was Indian or Pakistani, or something. Janice hoped that the bathrooms were clean.

The room cost $27 for the night. Janice had taken out $350.00 before she left New York. She knew that she could get more money from her folks. She didn't know what she would tell them, but she knew that if she were in trouble, they would do anything for her.

In any case, when Janice went to pay the $27.00, she handed the clerk a twenty and a ten. He declined payment. "Exact change after 10 P.M.," he said, pointing out a sign.

Janice looked at the sign. Yeah, that was what it said. "Shit!" she thought. She didn't want to use any credit cards in case they could be traced. "How about it if you keep the change?" she asked the clerk. He was a young kid, maybe 19. He was skinny and wore thick glasses. He pointed to another sign that read 'No Tipping.' He then pointed to a camera mounted on the wall behind Janice. She got the point.

She didn't want to drive to the next exit. It was getting late, and way out here she might not even find a motel office open. She was torn. She could sleep in her car, but it had gotten chilly when the sun went down and she was dressed very lightly. She could use a credit card, but maybe the company, or whoever they were that was after her would trace it.

Janice decided to give it a shot. If she used her credit card, the charge probably wouldn't get reported until the morning. By the time anyone could act, she would be almost home. Once she got home, she would call the FBI or something.

Janice was given Room 37. The double bed was covered by a dingy, pink flowered bedcover and the room smelt like nobody had opened the door for a week. Janice opened the windows to rid the room of its musty odor. She went into the bathroom and began to run the shower. The bathroom was ancient, with chipped, discolored tiles and a raggedy throw rug on the floor. But it was clean. That was what counted.

Janice waited until the room was aired out sufficiently and then she closed the windows and drew the drapes. It was only then that she got undressed for her shower. The water was plenty hot and she had to cool it a bit before stepping in. As she reached her hand in to test the water, she couldn't help but think of Janet Leigh in 'Psycho'. Would the Pakistani motel clerk come running in with a knife dressed in his mother's old sari? She doubted it. But she locked the bathroom door all the same.

When she finally had gotten ready for bed, she had dressed in clean panties and a tee shirt from her exercise bag. She went to sleep quickly.

Janice awoke to a loud knocking on the door. "Open up!" 'Bang! Bang! Bang!' "Open up. Police!"

Janice struggled to consciousness. She wasn't sure whether this was part of her dream or not. She had had the same dream as the night before, but this time she had been chased by men with badges. So the announcement that there were police at the door was somewhat confusing.

Janice had just thrown the covers off of her when the door came flying open. Daylight splashed into the darkened room. A brown uniformed policeman came barging in, gun drawn. He held it in front of him, his two hands joined on it and pointed it right at Janice's head. "Freeze!" he yelled.

Janice could do nothing else, she was so shocked. Another police officer came in behind the first and, circling him, pointed another gun at her. "Get down on the floor!" he yelled. Janice was not sure whether to freeze or get down on the floor. She glanced at the first policeman who looked like he was going to blow her head off. It took him a few seconds, but he finally got her message. "Down on the floor!" he yelled.

Trembling with fear, Janice lay down on the floor. Policeman Two yelled "Hands behind your back!" Janice complied immediately. Policeman Two approached her and locked her wrists together. Policeman One relaxed.

"Are you Janice Paterson?" the first policeman asked.

"Yes," Janice managed to squeak out. At first she was surprised that he had that information, but then realized that she had registered under her real name. And there was the credit card. When she remembered the credit card, she got a sinking feeling in her stomach.

"You're under arrest!"

Janice was stunned. "Arrest?" she said. "For what?"

"You'll get that down at the station, miss. Right now I'm going to assist you to get up and sit on the bed. Do you understand?" the officer advised her.

"Y,yes," she answered haltingly.

When she was sitting up on the bed, she noticed that the other cop was searching through her gym bag. "Hey!" she yelled. "What are you doing?"

Cop One said, "Shut up. He's searching your bag you stupid fuck."

"What for?" Janice asked

"You know, honey," the officer said. "Don't give us any shit. We want it now. This thing can go the easy way or the hard way. Not what'll it be?"

Incredulous, Janice replied, "I have no idea what you're talking about. I don't have anything. I just got here last…"

A vicious slap crossed Janice's face before she could finish the sentence. She fell down back on the bed, screeching in surprise. She turned to look at the officer who was standing between her legs. "I don't know what you mean, honest," she said. "You've made a mistake, I'm just here to…"

The police officer grabbed Janice by the hair and slapped her again. This time, his hand held her head steady and the entire blow was absorbed by her cheek. "Owwwwwwwwww!" Janice cried, tears running down her face. She had awoken from one nightmare to another.

The second cop yelled, "It's not here."

"Let's search the room," the first cop said. To Janice he said, "Get back down on the floor, cunt!"

He pulled Janice up by the hair and slammed her to the floor. Janice landed with a loud 'thump' and issued a comparable cry. The first cop took his own set of handcuffs and placed one end around her left ankle and connected the other end to the cuffs that confined her wrists. Janice was lying on the floor in her underwear, hands locked behind her and one leg in the air.

"Please, please," Janice cried. "Please tell me what this is all about!"

The first police officer did not respond, but, seeing her soiled underwear from the day before on the floor, he picked it up and jammed it into her mouth. "Shut the fuck up, cunt!" he yelled.

Now Janice, bound and silent, began to cry. The policemen turned everything in the room upside down and inside out. The mattress was thrown off of the bed, the closet was ransacked. It took them about two minutes to do the whole room.

"Maybe it's in the car," the first officer spoke.

The second one nodded and, seeing the car key on the dresser, he went outside. The first one took it upon himself to interrogate the suspect. He had put his gun away when he had seen Janice handcuffed, but he drew another instrument from his belt. He knelt down in front of Janice's head and whispered to her.

"Do you know what this is, cunt?"

Janice was unable to respond, but she did not know, in fact what it was.

"This is a Taser device. It sends out an electric shock. We use it to subdue recalcitrant suspects." He jammed it into Janice's ass and pulled the trigger. A painful shock shot through Janice's rear globe. She whined in pain.

"And," the officer continued, "it can be adjusted to give more power." He twisted a knob on its base. He jammed the device into Janice's other rear globe. 'Tszzzzzt!' the Taser spurted. Janice's whine was more of a howl, now as the tortuous tendrils from the electrical shock permeated her body.

"You see?" he queried her.

Janice nodded her head desperately. The cop pulled on Janice's confined leg until she was forced to turn over. The leg was jammed under her, straining her back. The other leg was free, but the officer quickly pulled it away and sat athwart it. Janice's precious sex was exposed, but for the thin layer of a pair of cotton panties, bikini type.

"I wonder what this would feel like, jammed up your cunt, bitch," the officer stated. Janice's eye's widened with fear. The second cop came back into the room.

"Not in the car.," he said neutrally. And then, more anxiously, "What're you doing?"

"Trying to get this bitch to talk, that's what I'm doing."

"Are you nuts? She goes and blabs that you were torturing her with your Taser and we're both up shit's creek. Listen," the second officer continued, "she could've dumped the money anywhere. She probably has some secret account that she can draw it from later or something. Or she hid it somewhere between here and New York."

"Jeez, Jake," the first officer responded, "$50,000 is $50,000."

"And getting charges against us is getting charges. Let's get her dressed and outta here. I'll have Connie notify New York that we've got her. And get that underwear out of her mouth, willya?"

When Janice reached the jail, she was locked in a holding cell in the rear of the station house. She had not been allowed to put on slacks or her socks and shoes. Her demands for a phone call to a lawyer, or to anyone else, for that matter, went unanswered.

As to the charges against her, all the police would tell her was that she had been charged with embezzling $50,000 from her employer. Apparently the APB that went out indicated that she had the cash on her, hence the frantic search by the arresting officers. If they had found it, it would never have reached the evidence room. Letting it be known that she had $50,000 in cash on her had provided extra incentive to have her picked up.

Janice's cell was five by ten. It had a little bench with a pad on it and a little toilet and sink. The station house did not have a separate area for female prisoners and so Janice had to suffer the taunts and catcalls from the dirt bags and derelicts in the neighboring cells. There was a female guard, but she just smirked when Janice asked for the rest of her clothes.

"I understand that you gave Miller and DeGrasso a hard time, honey. Maybe you'll think twice next time." Janice started to say that she hadn't given the officers a hard time when the guard left the cell block and shut the door.

The frightened and disoriented woman had not been allowed to pee at the motel and her bladder was near to bursting now. She had wanted to ask the guard if she could use a bathroom somewhere, but she had lost that chance. Red faced, she succumbed to the inevitable and pulled down her panties and sat on the toilet. The men in the cell block went wild. They hooted and hollered and made some rather salacious suggestions to her. The man in the next cell, a broken down old drunk, begged her to show him her tits.

"C'mon, honey, just a little peek," he said. "It can't hurt you ya know," he begged.

Janice was not prone to profanity, but there were no other words to describe how she felt. "Fuck you!" she said.

The hooting and hollering resumed. It intensified when she reached down to wipe herself and then stood to pull up her panties. She just walked over to the corner of her cell, crawled up into a ball and covered her head.

She had been told that she would get her rights when the New York Detectives came to pick her up. They arrived about 1 P.M. Janice knew they had arrived when the guard returned and told her to get up and that she was leaving. She asked again for her clothes but was told to 'shut up'. She was handcuffed and brought into the station proper. She was asked to sign certain forms, at which she balked.

"Listen, honey, you want to spend the next week back in there or you wanna get outta here?" the desk sergeant asked her.

She certainly didn't want to stay back there and so, after her wrists were freed, she signed. She was recuffed and led to a small conference room and shown in. Sitting there at the conference table, cups of coffee and doughnuts in their hands were Detectives Guray and Gower.

Janice was shocked. "No way is this a coincidence," she thought. She tried to back peddle out of the room, but she was too late. The door slammed behind her.

"I'm not going anywhere with you!" Janice announced. Det. Guray looked saddened.

"Listen, Ms. Paterson, we don't pick our assignments, we get assigned them. We were assigned to pick you up because we had had contact with you yesterday. We knew what you looked like. That's all."

Janice sputtered in her anger. "You bastards turned those pictures over to that company that's harassing me!" she accused. "I'm not going anywhere with you. I don't trust you!"

Guray again looked pained. "I don't know what you're talking about, Ms. Paterson. Those pictures went into our evidence files. They were private pictures. We wouldn't show them around. Besides, what makes you think that they were shown around?"

"I was emailed a copy of one," Janice answered angrily, "That's how!"

"By who?" Guray asked.

"By that company, you know, the one who's been harassing me," Janice replied. "I got it about two hours after I went to work."

"Now, Ms. Paterson," Guray said, trying to calm the young woman down. "I don't even know your email address. How could I send you a picture?"

"I don't know" Janice said, exasperated. "Maybe you gave them to the company. They seem to know everything about me."

"And I'm telling you that those pictures are sitting in my evidence cabinet in my office right now," Guray said angrily. "I don't like to be accused of something like that. For Christ's sake."

Doubt had reared its ugly head. Maybe these guys had nothing to do with it. "Does anyone else have access to your evidence cabinet Detective?" she inquired testily.

"Just my captain," Guray answered. Grower had sat there the whole time eating his donut and drinking his coffee. He now piped in.

"Just the captain. Even I don't have a key," he said.

Janice was still not certain. Suddenly, she realized that she was standing in front of these guys in her underwear. Her braless breasts were jiggling as she spoke, her nipples hard and pointed from fear. Grower was eying her crotch and tits surreptitiously. "Is somebody going to get me some pants or do I have to ride all the way to New York like this?" she asked, her voice rising.

"Relax, Ms. Paterson," Guray said. "We'll get you your pants. I guess these local boys had a little joke at your expense. But let's talk about these charges."

"I don't know anything about embezzling any money," Janice said.

"First," Guray said, "let me read you your rights." He read her her Miranda warnings and had her sign off on them.

"So why do you think someone made up these charges against you, Ms. Paterson," the detective continued.

A tear came to Janice's face. All throughout this ordeal she hadn't cried. But now, when the ultimate question had at last been asked, she couldn't take it any more. "I don't know," she cried. But she had some ideas. Maybe it was her boss. All those cash receipts he had her hand in for him. Were they bogus? But it was too much of a coincidence for that. Why did these charges come up now just when she was trying to leave from New York to get away from that company? Did they know everything about her? Janice decided she would wait until they got to New York so that she could speak to a lawyer.

"I'm not saying anything else," she told him.

"Suit yourself," he answered. "Now let's see if we can get your pants and get you out of here."

Janice got her pants and rode all the way back to New York in the rear of the unmarked police car without saying a word. She couldn't believe the mess she was in. Since she was charged with a crime, she would have to make bail. If she was on bail, she wouldn't be able to leave New York. Where would she go?

When they pulled over the George Washington Bridge and headed downtown, Det. Guray asked Janice if she would like to get some clean clothes before they took her to the Manhattan Detention Center at Riker's Island.

"Riker's Island?" she exclaimed. "I have to go to Riker's Island?"

"I'm afraid so, miss," Guray answered. "But we can stop at your place and get you some stuff if you want. I wouldn't want to be in their without clean skivvies and such," he said.

Janice was deflated. She had heard tales of that hellhole of a jail ever since she got to New York. Now she was going there herself. She realized that she needed more clean underwear than she had and some soap. She would probably think of some other things when she got to her apartment. She lifted her head. "Thank you, Det. Guray. I'd like to get a few things. But do I have to go in handcuffed?"

"I tell you what, Ms. Paterson, I'll handcuff you to my wrist, it'll look like we're holding hands. That is, unless you'd rather hold hands with Grower here?" he asked mirthfully.

"No, that's all right," Janice responded listlessly.

The car pulled up right outside her apartment building. Guray came around to the passenger side and, after Grower opened the door, unlocked one hasp of Janice's handcuffs and affixed it to his own wrist. He helped her out of the car.

They took the elevator up. Guray had taken Janice's keys from her property bag and he opened the door. He led Janice in, Grower followed.

It was then that Janice got the shock of her life. Sitting at her kitchen table, eating a big bowl of noodles, was the Asian guy from the day before, the one who had whipped her with his belt. Janice was speechless. In a trice, Guray had the handcuff off of his wrist and, with Growers' assistance, handcuffed her arms behind her back. Janice was just about to scream when Guray gave her a jab in the solar plexus. She collapsed to the floor, breathless. Guray and Grower stood over the gasping girl. She was making rasping sounds as she struggled for oxygen. The two detectives nodded knowingly to the muscle bound Asian and then turned and left.

Janice knelt on the floor, slowly regaining her breath. She looked up when she heard the door close behind her. The Asian man hadn't moved. He sat calmly at the table eating from a paper container of lo mien, snapping the round noodles up expertly with a pair of chopsticks. She was just about to stand and yell for help when the man gave her a fierce look. "Stay down," he said gruffly. "No talking!"

The young woman was overwhelmed. "All of this has been a ruse to get me back to my apartment!" she thought, forlornly. The embezzlement, the arrest warrant, the $50,000, everything. And now she was in the clutches of this fearsome hulk of a man, a man who had already whipped her. She started to cry.

The Asian man, who was, in fact, Korean, got up at this point. Janice didn't know if it was because she had started to cry or because he had finished eating his noodles. It didn't matter. He was coming for her. The first thing he did was pull her to her feet by her hair. Janice grimaced and wailed at the pain. He then took a roll of tape from his pocket and tore off a long piece. The tape was about 4" wide. He placed it over Janice's mouth.

Janice realized that her last, best chance to get away from this giant had gone. She should have been jumping up and down screaming her head off. He would have subdued her eventually, but someone might have heard. "And done what?" she thought to herself miserably, "Called the police?"

勢霸

CHAPTER THREE
A NIGHT IN NEW YORK

The huge Korean dragged Janice into the bedroom by her hair and threw her on the bed. She scrambled, trying to get away from him, but he grabbed her leg and held it high in the air. He turned and dropped her on the floor. Janice's shoulder hit the floor first with a loud 'thump' and she moaned in pain. The Korean again grabbed her hair and again threw her on the bed. Again Janice struggled to get away from him. And again he lifted her leg up in the air, turned and dropped her on the floor. This time she landed on her other shoulder. She winced in pain. When he threw her on the bed the third time, she stayed.

The man pushed Janice to her back. With one hand on her chest, holding her down, he used the other to undo her belt and pull down the zipper to her slacks. Janice was limp with fear. She was going to be raped right here in her own bedroom during the middle of the afternoon. She was powerless to stop it. She couldn't yell for help. And the man had well proven his physical mastery of her. To continue to struggle meant only unnecessary pain.

Janice couldn't decide whether to fight him or to cooperate. If she cooperated, he might not hurt her. If she fought him, there was little or no chance she could resist him, but she might preserve part of her pride. Was it worth it? Janice decided not. She desperately wanted to avoid pain.

The man pulled her jeans and underwear down over her hips and down to her ankles. When her pants and panties were pulled free from her feet, the Korean grabbed both of her long, graceful legs and wrapped them together with the duct tape. The frantic girl was confused. Why tape her legs together if he was going to rape her? Did he have something else in mind?

The Korean pulled Janice back up to a sitting position by the hair. She winced from the pain. The roots of her hair burned from the man's abuse. He unlocked the handcuffs and motioned for her to take off her t-shirt. Janice had not had time to put on a bra that morning, and the police had not condescended to give her one. So, the removal of her t-shirt meant that her bare breasts would be exposed to the man's view. But that seemed of little moment, since he had already seen her naked, hairy bush, the fulcrum of her well toned thighs. She reluctantly pulled the t-shirt over her head and dropped it on the floor. She looked fearfully up at the giant of a man.

The Asian man pushed Janice face down on the bed and grabbed her arms. He taped her wrists together behind her back, pulling sharply, causing her shoulder muscles to strain and drawing a moan from the anxious girl.

Janice was seized with fear. She tried to struggle at her bonds, desperate now to avoid whatever fate this man had in store for her. But it was too late. The opportunity for escape, if there ever was one, was past. Janice's stomach churned and heaved with dread as two short pieces of tape were placed over her eyes, blinding her.

The man pulled Janice's legs up and wound more tape around her ankles. He then took hold of her bound wrists and connected them to her ankles with the tape, effectively hog tying her. Janice could feel the tape being wound around her ankles and wrists many times, and she wondered, fearfully, what was the man's purpose. She felt her body lifted from the bed, the man taking hold of her bound wrists and ankles and lifting her up. Once off of the bed, he lowered her body and dragged her across the floor by her feet, her nipples and breasts rubbing harshly against the less than plush rug, sending a burning irritation through them.

Janice's apartment was a converted pre-war luxury hotel. Many of the rooms had been chopped up. But the walls and doorframes carried fine, antique moldings. The door to the bathroom had a lintel at the top and a transom window. The Asian dumped Janice at the entrance to the bathroom. She could hear his belt being removed from his trousers and she whined as she anticipated another round of whippings. But the Asian had something else in mind. He lifted Janice's body up again, this time bringing her bound wrists and ankles to the level of his shoulder. He looped the belt over the transom and through the gap between Janice's bound limbs. He closed the belt and slowly lowered Janice until her melded wrists and ankles were lifted up behind her. He then released her body, allowing her to swing free.

The poor girl moaned with pain as all of her weight came to rest on her shoulders and hips. The Asian gave her head a little push and she swung back and forth, causing shoots of pain to course through her body. Her breasts dangled in slow movement. She begged and pleaded behind her taped lips to be freed. She could hear the Korean's heavy tread as he walked back to the dining area. There was the sound of the chair legs scraping along the vinyl tiles and then the unmistakable sound of the Korean continuing his meal.

Janice, of course, had no way to know how long she hung there, her shoulder muscles stretched to their extreme, her hips aching with the strain. Her neck muscles burned and she could find no comfortable position for her head, whether hung down towards the floor or lifted up. She heard the man turn on the television and tune in a foreign language channel. It must have been a comedy show, because she heard him laugh heartily several times. Janice found nothing funny about her predicament. She sobbed and cried her chest heaving with misery, her bare, melon sized breasts swinging freely beneath her.

After a considerable time, she heard the man walking across the floor towards her, and her heart leapt as she imagined that he was coming to free her. But she felt her body shoved aside and heard the man lift the seat of the toilet behind her. He took a long, noisy piss. She heard the toilet flush and the sounds of the man washing up. He paused as he stepped near her. Janice knew that her legs were splayed wide open and she was mortified that this man was enjoying a bird's eye view of her private places. Her limbs were too sore for her to try and twist and turn in protest.

She felt the man step nearer and place his hands on the insides of her thighs. Her legs were pushed wide apart, increasing the painful pressure on her shoulders, back and hips. She was too weak to resist. The man's hands were surprisingly soft as they ran the length of her tender upper legs. Janice tried to ignore the warmth that spread to her loins from the man's intimate touch.

The man pushed Janice's thighs even wider apart and placed his hands on either side of her now glistening slit.

Pulling on the skin, he drew apart the delicate lips that concealed her pink, moist interior. Janice shuddered as she felt his tongue trace the distance from her perineum to the apex of her labial divide. A tingling ran through her body as the stiff, hard tongue teased her dainty bud.

"No, no, no!" the frantic girl thought to herself, mortified that this cruel man could induce her to pleasure. Although her body was wracked with pain, her lusts began to rise. She didn't want this, to be so grossly treated by this rough, callous man. She could feel the invasive tongue delve deep into her crevasse, the mouth encompassing her sensitive nether lips.

The Asian reveled in the musky smell and tart flavor of Janice's slowly engorging cunt. When he seized Janice's clit with his teeth, nipping at it gently, tugging it outwards, the girl moaned with unwanted pleasure. The man began to lick the length of Janice's throbbing gash, his tongue collecting her oozing discharge. Soon the painful aches of Janice's hips and shoulders subsided in her consciousness as her passion began to overwhelm her.

"Not this!" she thought desperately. "Not this!" Janice dreaded the loss of control over her sexual release. She was used to carefully managing her orgasms, opting for the smooth, warm overflow of pleasure to the lustful abandonment of all rational control. But it was the Asian who was in control, it was he who would determine how Janice would take her orgasm. Her mind revolted at the thought of her body convulsing in unrestrained passion in the presence of and at the behest of this strange, cruel man.

The girl tried to resist the waves of pleasure that washed over her, the product of the man's ardent tongue. Her breath became labored; her thoughts began to cloud over. The man buried his tongue and lips in Janice's cunt and reached out beneath her, grabbing her dangling breasts. One squeeze was all it took, and Janice was spinning out of control. Her sex pulsed with heavy, intense contractions of pleasure. She moaned loudly, all of her concentration on the man's knowledgeable assault on her breasts and cunt. "Ohhhhhhhhhhh!" she moaned as her body shuddered with each electric pulse of pleasure. She tried futilely to close her thighs as she convulsed with each contraction of her pussy's walls, but the man's tongue continued to torment her, driving her orgasm on and on.

The Asian abandoned his efforts only when he was sure that Janice's spasms had subsided. He rose to his full height, wiping her copious discharge from his face with his sleeve. He reached under the girl and pinched her nipples harshly, causing Janice to jolt at the unexpected pain. He stepped past her dangling form and, as he went to return to his television show, he gave Janice's head another little push, causing her helpless form to again sway back and forth, like some strange, obscene pendulum.

It seemed to Janice like an hour or so later that she heard the giant man approach her once again. She felt her body sway slightly and then begin to be lowered from her perch. She was grateful for the release. He unfastened her wrists from her ankles, freeing her from her hog tie. Her muscles screamed with pain as their strained and extended states were relieved. The tape covering her eyes was removed. The man then tore off the tape around her ankles and, after lifting her to her feet, sat her roughly down on the toilet.

Janice didn't need to be told twice what to do. Her bladder was near bursting. The fluid fled from her body in a steady stream. When she was done, the Asian lifted her from the seat by her hair and made her spread her legs so that she could be cleaned of her liquid wastes.

Just then there was a knock on the door. The Korean stopped what he was doing. The buzzer to the apartment rang. He dragged Janice into the living room and, after considering his options, opened the hallway closet and pushed her in.

"You make noise, you very sorry," he told her in his pigeon English. Janice nodded. She believed that this cruel, mammoth man could make her very sorry indeed. He could probably kill whoever was at the door and then return to extinguish her life in an instant.

Standing in the close darkness of the closet, Janice heard the door to the apartment opening. She heard a voice. "Twenty-two fifty," a nasal, young, male voice said. And then a moment later, "Thanks."

Janice was stunned. The Asian fellow had ordered out for more food! A tear rolled down her cheek as she thought of her own hungry stomach that now, because she was no longer dealing with the pain of being hung from a lintel, began to gnaw at her.

She had been shoved back against the coats and other odds and ends that were hanging there. Her bare feet had to shuffle to avoid tripping over the shoes and boots. Her bound hands could feel the fabric of the clothing behind her. When she leaned forward, her breasts and face touched on the inside of the door. The shelf above the clothes was a little over 5' high and it banged against her head whenever she moved.

The closet door was hollow and she could hear the television from the living room, the tinny Asian voices a taunting reminder that she was under the control of a hostile, foreign force. From time to time, as she stood silently in her small prison, she could also hear sounds of life throughout the apartment building. The Jamisons downstairs were fighting again, their voices exchanging rants muted by the floor beneath her feet. Somewhere there was a radio playing. She heard the flush of a toilet.

Maybe, she thought, if she banged the walls someone would hear and come to investigate. But the giant behemoth who had invaded her apartment would hear it as well. She heard him laughing at his Asian TV sitcom. Maybe the television would be too loud for him to hear her banging? She could pound on the floor with her foot. The last time the Jamisons were at it, she had knocked on the floor with the handle of a broom. Old man Jamison came running upstairs all pissed off to remonstrate with her. Maybe he would do it again?

But then Janice imagined her tormentor snapping her neck in two just before he ran out the door and smashed Mr. Jamison's face. It was not a pretty thought. No, she would remain quiet. Somehow she would be able to escape, she hoped.

The evening waned into lateness before the Korean came to release Janice from the closet. Her feet and legs ached from standing for what must have been over three hours. She had spent the time cursing her fate, wondering what she had ever done to deserve this, and ruing that simple little phone call she had made two days ago.

She also thought of her friend, Denise. That was the explanation for the perfunctory letter she had received. Denise was their prisoner too! But she was on the West Coast. A twist formed in the pit of Janice's stomach as she contemplated how large and how powerful the organization that had entrapped her might really be.

After being released from the closet, she was allowed to pee again. The Asian sat her down at the kitchen table. He had eaten all but a very small portion of the General Tso's chicken and the pork fried rice. There were escaped grains of rice and smears of sauce all over the table. Janice was a fastidious housekeeper and was pissed off that this animal would make such a mess of her apartment. Her whole life had been invaded. Anger welled up in her. What right did this man have to treat her this way? What right did these people have to pursue her, to ruin her life? She glared at the man as the wiped his face and greasy hands with a paper napkin, looking back at her with insolence and amusement.

The man reached out and abruptly tore off the tape that had muted Janice's voice for many hours. The sundering of the adhesive bond with her skin was exquisitely painful. Janice uttered a whine at the rough treatment. Rage formed in her eyes as she absorbed this new insult. The Korean looked at her. His brow furrowed.

"No talk, eat," he said in his deep, raspy voice. Janice felt her eyes moisten, her resolve to protest weaken under the cruel man's stark gaze. She was sitting nude in her own kitchen, her hands bound behind her, and this man was surprised that she might cry out if he hurt her? She nodded her head meekly in understanding and then looked down at the remnants of the Asian man's meal. She couldn't feed herself and she was ravenously hungry. She looked up at the Korean. In response, he shoved the round plastic container that held the chicken in front of her and spilled the rest of the rice in it. "Eat," was all he said.

Janice got the idea that the man wanted her to place her face in the bowl and eat from it like an animal. She looked up at the man. He was looking at her. There were chopsticks on the table. Janice looked at them and back at the man pleadingly. She tried to murmur an almost silent request. Seeing her lips beginning to form a word, the man repeated his earlier formulation, but in a much firmer voice, "No talk, eat!"

Janice looked down at the circular plastic bowl. Her stomach churned with ravenous demand. She was very hungry. She would get hungrier if she didn't eat. Who knows when he'll offer me food again, she wondered to herself.

The naked and bound prisoner gave up her dignity and plunged her face into the bowl. She picked up a piece of chicken with her teeth and started to chew on it. She got the piece about halfway down when the fire alarm went off. Her mouth and throat burned like the blazes. "Oh! Oh!" she called out, chicken and rice spilling from her mouth.

"Oh! Oh!" she cried again as the spicy fire from the food raged inside her oral cavity. The Korean was beside himself. He gave out a great belly laugh. Janice stood abruptly from her chair, knocking it down to the floor, and rushed about the room, frantically looking for some liquid with which to put out the blazing fire in her mouth. "Oh! Oh!" she repeated. The Korean rose from the chair and, smiling, pulled the roll of duct tape from his pocket. Janice saw him tearing off a six inch long strip.

"Oh, please!" she begged frantically, her voice a little over a whisper. "Pleases give me something to drink, please!"

Grinning from ear to ear, the Korean backed Janice into a corner. "No talk, eat!" he said again and then burst into another round of mirthful laughter. Janice contemplated yelling and screaming. But she waited just a moment too long. In a flash, with a quickness of movement that astonished the girl, she found her lips resealed with the duct tape. She had never seen anyone's hands move so fast and was astonished to see it from such a huge, apparently ungainly man.

"Mmmmmmmmmf!" she called out, remembering her scorched throat and mouth. The Korean grabbed her by her hair and towed her across the apartment. He brought her back to the bathroom door. Pushing her to the floor, he rewrapped her ankles together. Janice cried and struggled as she was bound. The burning of her mouth had begun to subside, but the humiliation of the cruel trick the man had played her and his mocking, insulting laughter was still sinking in. The man had made a fool of her. He had had played a sadistic joke, inviting her to degrade herself by eating like some dog or cat from a bowl and then laughing at her extreme distress.

When Janice's ankles were rebound, the man lifted them upwards. He took his belt again and ran it through the gap between her shins. Janice heard him pull the belt tightly closed around the transom and then let go of her legs. She was hanging upside down in the bathroom doorway, her face towards the living area of the apartment. The Korean gave the inverted girl a loud smack on her ass with his frying pan sized hand. He walked away laughing to himself.

Janice's naked body swung gently to and fro as a result of the stinging slap. She shook and moaned in unhappy, miserable frustration. She looked upon her upside down apartment, her private space. The Korean had sat himself down again in front of the TV. The detritus of his meal lay scattered across the kitchen table. It was almost surreal, being treated this strange way in her most familiar surroundings. It was clear to Janice that this man could do almost anything he wanted to her. Why hadn't he raped her? What was the point of all this? What did the people who had sent this tormenting hulk of a man want from her?

As the evening wore on, Janice's legs and back began to ache. She was afraid that the man would make her hang upside down all night. Her head was aching from the pressure of her blood and it was beginning to become difficult to breathe. The man had fallen asleep watching some kind of cartoons. Janice could hear him snoring. She had tried desperately to free herself, but she was taped too tightly. She resigned herself to awaiting whatever fate this man intended for her.

Finally, something awoke the Asian and he shuffled over to where Janice hung listlessly from her feet. She was moaning lowly as the man released her ankles and lowered her to the floor. She was dragged across the rug again, its rough surface scratching and tearing at her flesh, and was lifted onto her bed. Her arms and legs were unbound. She felt the man grab her hair behind her head and pull her head back rudely. As he lifted it, he spoke with a low, threatening voice into her face.

"No trouble," he growled. "Tomorrow you take limousine. Understand?"

Janice nodded her head miserably. To say that she was dispirited would be to belittle the physical and emotional abyss into which she had fallen, into which this giant, ruthless, sadistic man had delivered her.

Janice heard the man's steps move away from her and the door to her apartment open and then slam shut as the Asian inexplicably left. She buried her head in the pillow and cried.

勢覇

CHAPTER FOUR
A FATEFUL TRIP

Janice hardly slept. What do these people want from me? she thought miserably, her face buried in her pillow, the covers pulled up over her head. When the Asian man had left, she cried for an hour. She had never been treated so cruelly. It was about 2 A.M. when she was finally able to gather herself. She knew that she couldn't call the police. She dared not call any of her friends lest they get mixed up in this. She was sure that the phone was tapped. That also left out her mother or her sister in Ashtabula. She could just take off and run, but she had no money and no means of transportation. And where would she go? She realized dismally that she really had no choice but to obey the Asian man's instructions.

It was almost dawn when Janice finally nodded off. Seven o'clock came soon afterwards. Ruefully, she got up and showered. She ate a small breakfast and dressed. She wore a plain light blue cotton work skirt that descended to just below her knees and a windowpane plaid blouse, white with dark blue and black lines. She put on her makeup and brushed her hair like any other work day. But it wasn't any other work day. Three times she had to renew her mascara due to the fact that her eyes kept filling up with tears. Her stomach was in a knot. She cleaned up the apartment and threw the discarded strands of duct tape, evidence that her memories of the day before were real and not a nightmare, into the garbage.

At exactly 8:15, Janice walked down the stairs to the ground floor. She hesitated before going out to the street. From her vantage point in the large foyer, she could see the black limo parked right outside the glass doors to the building. The small uniformed chauffeur was leaning on the door to the car. She saw him look at his watch. People from her building were streaming out of the elevators and dashing outside to catch their bus, subway or taxi to work. Janice felt like her feet were planted in cement. She knew that somehow, when she entered the long, black Lincoln, her life would change inalterably. But to what? It was all so absurd that it was almost laughable.

Janice looked at her watch. It was now 8:20. She didn't want to go through another day of abuse by the huge Asian man. That was what put her over the top, the tipping point between her fear of action and inaction. Maybe if she toughed it out, made it clear that she was unsuitable for whatever they wanted her for, they would let her go, she thought. With a mighty effort, Janice forced her right leg forward.

As she walked through the glass doors of her apartment building, the uniformed man saw her. He straightened up and smiled. He opened the rear door of the limo for her. As she went to step in, the man grabbed her arm lightly. "Sorry, missy," he said. "Purse must go up front."

Janice's purse contained her whole life, her identification, her money, her cell phone. It had in it all of the accouterments used and useful by a twenty first century single woman in New York City. She would no more part with it, under normal circumstances, than take off her dress. It was as much a part of her as her shoes. But this was not a normal circumstance. For a second, Janice thought of running away. But the man read her mind and the grip on her arm became more firm.

"Missy must follow rules," the driver said ominously. "Please to give me handbag and get in car," he said sternly.

Reluctantly, Janice let go of her bag and entered the back seat of the Lincoln. The moment that she sat down, the door slammed shut. The vehicle had a luxurious interior. But Janice noted right away that the windows were so heavily tinted that she could not see out. There was a divider between the front and back seats and that was tinted too. As she heard the front door of the limo open and close, the young woman panicked. What am I doing? she thought frantically. She went to reach for the door handle so that she could get out and run, but the handles had been removed. The frightened woman raised her small fist to bang on the window to attract attention, to get help. The car pulled quickly away from the curb. Her body was thrown back on the seat.

Janice could sense that the limo was being driven very fast. It was in the city, so it had to stop every time and again, and each time that it did, she started to yell and scream while banging on the side window. She even took her high heel and slammed it against the glass. But either no one heard or no one cared. The car would start again and she would sit back in despair.

It was about 45 minutes later that the van slowed and seemed to pull into some kind of driveway or garage. It was a garage, and the car did not stop until it had dropped three levels below the street. The driver hopped out and opened Janice's door. The frightened girl emerged cautiously. There was a door opposite the passenger side of the limo and the driver was pointing to it and urging her out of the vehicle.

"Missy must go through door," he said. "Quick! Quick! You bad girl, very late!"

Janice's face cringed as she tried to screw up the courage to leave the vehicle. She knew that if she didn't get out, the driver would either take her out himself by force or call some other men to do it for him. She had no idea where she was except that she knew that she was somewhere in the City. Maybe I'm at that Third Avenue address on the envelope? She thought to herself. But she realized that that could just be an office address or a mail drop. She could be in Brooklyn, the Bronx or Queens. Maybe even Yonkers! Or, god forbid, New Jersey! Not to know where she was made her doubly fearful to go through the door that the driver was pointing to.

"Out! Out!" the man shouted at her. His voice echoed through the empty garage basement. Janice's stomach turned as she realized that she was wholly subject to this man's power. Not only did she not know where she was, no one else did either. She could just disappear off the face of the earth!

Finally, the young girl stepped out of the car. Her skirt rode high on her thigh as she stretched out her right leg. The driver looked at it and smiled. He bowed and waived his hand at the door.

"M,my purse, please," Janice managed to squeak out, not quite as assertive as she had hoped.

"No need purse," the man replied. "Please to go inside."

With great foreboding, Janice walked over to the shiny steel door. She grabbed the black doorknob and turned it. The door opened easily. On the other side of the door was a short corridor and another door, a standard office type door with a brass doorknob. Janice let the steel door shut behind her. She turned and noticed that there was no interior handle. She had no choice but to go on. She stepped nervously down the hall and turned the knob of the wooden door. It opened to a small sitting area, with a small sofa and a side table. There was a glass partition covering one half of a wall. A brown haired, pale skinned young woman sat behind it. She was on the telephone. She opened the sliding glass.

"I'll be right witcha," she said. She was chewing gum and had on bright red lipstick and dark eyeliner. Her hair was done up on her head like some bimbo from the Fifties. She was wearing a bright yellow halter top. A gold chain dangled around her neck. It was not what Janice expected.

She took a seat on the sofa. There was nothing to read and so she bided her time until the receptionist was finished with her call.

Suddenly the glass window slid open again. The girl, about 24 or 25, handed out a clipboard. "Please fill out the forms. Let me know when you're done," the young lady said.

Janice took the clipboard and sat tentatively back down on the couch. She looked at the top. Her name, address, social security number and other vital information was already typed in. Underneath was a series of questions, some with blanks and some designed to allow the person completing it to check off yes or no or to select from a list of options.

The first two questions were fairly mundane. Married or not; children or not. But the second two were much more intrusive: virgin or not; heterosexual, homosexual or bisexual.

Janice looked up at the receptionist. The girl was paying her no heed. Janice looked down at the next few questions. 'Age of first sexual experience. Describe.' There was an open space for about three sentences. The next question was, 'How many sexual partners have you had?' There was a spot for hetero partners, homosexual partners and group sex. Janice got up from the sofa. She knocked on the glass. The girl slid the window open.

"I'm not answering these questions," she told the girl sternly. Somehow the mundane appearance of the girl and the waiting room had given Janice new found courage.

"Suit yourself, miss," the girl said. "But if I was three days late, I wouldn't want to piss anyone off. You know what I mean?"

"I don't care what you think," Janice retorted. "I'm not filling out this form."

"Fine," the girl snipped back. She closed the window and picked up the phone. Janice could hear her tell someone that, "the lady won't fill in the questionnaire." She saw the girl nod twice. "Okay," she said. She opened the window again.

"Come in and go to the third door on your left. Someone will be with you shortly." A buzzer sounded and the door to the interior of the office popped open.

"What should I do with this?" Janice asked, holding up the questionnaire.

"Give it to me, sweetie," the girl said.

Janice stepped through the door and entered a long, red carpeted hallway. She counted three doors down on her left and entered the room. There was a small divan in the middle of it, a long sofa and an armoire set against the wall. The sofa and ottoman were white. The rug was a dull brown and the armoire was made of a blonde stained oak.

There were overhead florescent lights. The door closed behind Janice as she entered the room. She turned when she heard the bolt click closed. No handle.

There was a sign on the wall with large, black block letters that said, "Please undress and put your clothes in a locker." The wall opposite the armoire was lined with doorless lockers. Several of them were filled with women's clothes. Janice's stomach curdled at the thought of undressing in this strange place. Who knew who would be next through the door? Janice determined that she would not do anything else until someone explained to her what was up.

She was sitting on the couch when the door opened. A large boned, heavy set, middle aged woman entered. She was about 5'10" tall. She had a ruddy face, short, curly brown hair and was dressed in a white shirtwaist dress, almost like a nurse. She wore white tights and white sneakers. The only thing she was missing was the little cap. She looked at Janice with annoyance. Janice stood up when she entered.

"Didn't you see the sign?" she asked, her irritation evident in her voice.

Janice was taken aback by the fearsome aspect of the woman, but she held her ground. "I'm not doing anything until someone explains to me what this is all about," she said. "I've been arrested, assaulted in my own home,..." She started to say. But the words were barely out of her mouth when the large woman stepped up to her and grabbed her hair at the back of her head. Janice flinched and then grimaced in pain. "Ow!" she yelled.

The older woman dragged Janice by her hair to the back of the couch. "Let me go!" Janice yelled. "What are you doing?" She felt her head pulled over the back of the couch until she was bent in two over it. The woman's grip was like a trap of steel. Janice tried flailing her hands, but she couldn't resist the woman's superior force. The woman grabbed the hem of Janice's skirt and raised it, capturing it with the thumb of the hand holding her hair. The angry and determined woman took a pen-like device from her pocket. With a click of a button, a long, thin, steel wand popped out. Janice's plain white cotton panties and her pantyhose clad legs were displayed. The woman reared back her arm and struck.

Janice howled as the thin, steel wand burned into the rear of her thighs. In three more rapid strokes, the whip-like rod was applied to her buttocks twice and again to the back of her legs. She screamed and yelled as each one landed. It was like lines of fire had crossed over her body. The woman released her and she fell to the floor, sobbing.

"Get up and get undressed!" the woman ordered churlishly.

Janice was crying and moaning. She stared wide eyed at the woman. She realized that she was in a whole world of shit. "Okay! Okay!" she said, crawling out of range of the woman's baton. "I'll do it!"

She pushed herself to her feet and started to unbutton her blouse. Her fingers fumbled at the buttons, but she was able to manage it. Her hands were sweaty with fear. She hung the blouse on one of the hooks in an empty locker. She kicked off her shoes and pulled her ripped pantyhose off of her legs. Her thighs and rear still stung from the blows she had received and she watched the older woman warily.

The frightened, crying girl hesitated at removing her skirt. "Come on! Come on!" the woman yelled.

With a sob, Janice unzipped the skirt at its side and let it drop to the floor. She stepped out of it and it joined the blouse in the locker. Under the glare of the older woman's eyes, she removed her bra, unleashing her ample orbs. She turned slightly so that she could obscure the woman's view. The skin over her breasts was taut with fear and her nipples had hardened. There was only one more thing to remove, and Janice looked at the woman as if to plead for an exemption. The woman just stared back. "Turn around!" she ordered. "Don't you think I've seen a pair of tits before?"

Obediently, Janice turned to face the woman. Screwing up her courage, she locked her thumbs in the elastic of her underwear and pulled them down her thighs and down to her ankles. She stepped out of them and hung them on a hook. Tearfully, stark naked, she turned to her oppressor.

"Put your hands behind your head!" the matronly woman ordered.

Janice was stunned by this instruction. She already felt as vulnerable and exposed as she had ever felt. The world was divided into people with clothes and those without; those with power, dignity and self determination, and those without. She had just shifted classes and her stomach churned with dire portent. Raising her arms would elevate and make prominent her plump, white breasts. She looked at the steel wand that the woman still wielded. She obeyed.

The naked, young woman stood in the middle of the room, her eyes jammed shut, trying to block out what was happening to her. Her breasts rose up prominently before her. She trembled in apprehension, making the tips of her breasts jiggle slightly. Janice heard the older woman, her assailant, open the cabinet on the far wall and then step back to where she stood. She sensed her going around her back. "Don't move, slut," the woman ordered.

Slut? Janice thought to herself. Why did she call her that? She hadn't done anything to warrant that label. She felt something circling her wrist. It was some kind of leather bracelet. She tried to see it from the corner of her eye. Another bracelet was affixed to her other wrist. As the woman pulled her arms down from behind her head, Janice realized that there was only one explanation for the bracelets. She was going to bind her hands behind her back!

Unfortunately for Janice, her realization came about a second or two too late. She felt her wrists clipped together. Before she was frightened. Now she was scared. "Please," she whispered to the woman, "what's going to happen to me?"

"You'll find out soon enough," the woman spat back. Janice felt a wide, thick leather collar affixed around her neck. It fit tightly around it. She heard a 'click' as it closed shut. "Turn around," the woman ordered her churlishly.

Janice felt the woman's hands on her shoulders forcing her to present her front to her. There was a thick leather plug in her hands. Janice realized what it was for. "Oh, please don't gag me," she said forlornly, a deep whine in her voice. "I'll be quiet, I promise."

"Shut up, cunt," the woman said. "Open your mouth."

Janice began to back away from the woman. "No, please. Please let me go. I don't want to be here; it's some kind of mistake," she protested. "I don't want to be gagged!" she cried.

The woman relentlessly followed Janice until she was backed up against the wall. Janice's eyes focused on the gag as if it were a snake about to leap at her. When her back hit the wall, she moaned in dismal unhappiness. The woman pressed the leather instrument to her lips. Tears flowed down the girl's face. As the pressure built against her teeth, Janice realized that she would have to bow to the inevitable. With a desperate groan, she opened her mouth and let the thick plug in.

The matron buckled the gag tightly behind Janice's head. "Follow me," she ordered and she used a key to unlock the door to the room. She opened the door and signaled Janice to walk out. Janice stared at her with alarm. There were people out there. She was naked. She would rather die first than to be seen all trussed up and walking around in the nude. She shook her head and backed up into the room. The matron frowned. "We're not going to go through this again," she said. She pulled the wand from her pocket and snapped it open.

Janice tried to protest the use of the whip like steel on her body. "Nnnnnnnnnn!" she called out, her voice muffled by the gag. The matron swung the wand viciously at Janice's legs, her hips and her arms. The wand made a 'zipping' noise as it cut through the air. Bright red lines rose up where the girl was struck. "Oooooooooogh! Oooooooooogh!" Janice cried out in alarm and pain as she tried to shy away from the blows. "Oooooooooough!" Janice moaned as she slid to the floor, crunching her body into a little ball to escape the painful lashes.

After five strokes of the wand, the matron relented. "Next time it'll be on your tits," she said. "Now, get up and no more problems. Got it?" the matron said menacingly.

Janice, crying from the pain and humiliation, nodded her head. She worked herself to her knees and stood. The matron again walked to the door and held it open. Meekly, her face wet with tears, Janice followed the white clad woman and then stepped out into the hall.

At the end of the hall was another door. The matron opened it with her key and motioned Janice through it. The door opened into a large office. The walls were white and it was divided into three cubicles by 4' high partitions. Calendars, charts and other business papers were mounted on the walls. Three well dressed, young, pretty Asian women were sitting in front of computer consoles. Two of them were on the telephone. They all had almost identically cut, shoulder length black hair. One wore gold wire rimmed glasses.

At first, none of the girls looked up. Janice was mortified, nonetheless, as she stood there nude and bound. The matron grabbed her arm and marched her into the middle of the room. Janice's thoughts of resistance were squelched by the firmness of the woman's grip and the memory of the pain brought by the application of the matron's steel wand. As she was passing through the room, one of the girls looked up and spoke to the others, not in English, but in what Janice presumed to be Japanese or Chinese. The other girls looked up and tittered. Janice turned red with embarrassment.

The matron led Janice to a doorway that opened into to a room that looked like a doctor's examination room. There was a scale, an examination table, clean white counters and a medicine cabinet.

"Now let's see what you're all about," the matron said in an officious manner. "Get up on the scale."

Timidly, Janice stepped forwards. She stepped up and the matron slid the weights along the top. "One hundred twenty seven pounds," she said. "Just a little tubby, dearie," she told the unhappy girl. She pinched the 1" role of flesh from Janice's hips. "You'll have to work on that," she said almost gleefully.

The matron had picked up a clipboard with a white form on it and entered the weight in the appropriate spot. She turned Janice around on the scale and measured her height. Janice stood 5'7" in her bare feet. Not too tall and not too short. The matron unlocked Janice's hands from behind her and commenced another series of measurements. She measured her hips, her breasts, both around her chest and their size, across, up and down and around. She measured the length of her legs and the circumference around her wrists and ankles, the lengths of her arms and across her shoulders.

Janice cooperated with the broad shouldered woman without complaint. She had already experienced he consequences of disobedience. But she found it strange that the woman needed such precise measurements of virtually every aspect of her body.

After the measurements were finished, the matron took blood and urine samples from the girl, making her squat and pee into a bottle, and then, when it was full, into a bedpan she shoved underneath her. Janice was mortified to have to urinate in front of this strange woman. But embarrassment was better than pain.

The matron then had Janice hop up onto the examination table. She measured her heartbeat and blood pressure while taking her temperature. Janice was then forced to lay back on the table. The matron took her wrists and fastened them to a ring at the top. It was a most thorough examination. And so Janice was not surprised when the matron pulled two stirrups from the sides of the table and placed her heels in them. She was a little disconcerted when she felt them strapped in.

Janice's legs were spread wide and the woman took her time examining the folds of her sex. She removed a speculum from a plastic bag and, with a little flashlight peered deep inside the girl. She took two swabs.

"Okay, dearie," the matron said in a singsong voice, "almost done." She went behind Janice and made an adjustment to the examination table. The top of the table on which Janice's torso lay began to rise. It was hinged in the middle so that her bottom remained still. Janice could hear the ratcheting sounds as the woman used some kind of a pedal to lift it up. She was sitting up, her hands raised above her head locked to the top edge of the table as the woman looked into her eyes and ears. The gag came off and the woman looked in her mouth, lifting the tongue with a depressor and then pushing it down to take a good look at her throat. Janice did not protest as the gag was returned to her mouth. The woman buckled a strap across Janice's chest, pressing her back against the raised top.

All along, the matron had kept making little notations on her clipboard. She went over to the counter out of Janice's view and then returned with some sort of apparatus. In sat on top of a little cart. The woman placed electrodes on Janice's chest, as if she were going to give the girl an EKG. When she had done that, she smiled at Janice and walked to the door. She opened it and called out to the three Asian women who were still at their computer stations. Janice could not understand what she said because it was in Japanese. When the matron turned back into the room, she was followed by the three young women. They had rolled their secretarial chairs into the room and, after they arranged them at the base of the examination table, they sat down in them.

The women seemed to be just about as amused as Janice was perturbed. Her legs were spread, her heels locked into the stirrups of the table, her hairy sex exposed for all to see. Janice whined and struggled in protest. The matron ignored her and brought the strange device between her legs. She raised her head to see what it was, but the matron pushed her head back down. "Sit still, cunt," she said harshly. She had a black sleeping mask in her hands and she stretched the elastic behind Janice's head and pulled the mask over her eyes. Everything went black.

Janice could hear the three young Asian girls giggling as the matron pushed the device closer to her sex. She felt a pad of some kind pressed against the apex. Straps went around her upper thighs. The rest of the device pressed up against and surrounded her slit. The helpless young girl squirmed as she felt the coolness of the steel. The device was cinched tight against her. There was a moment's pause and the girl felt an object being pressed against the lips of her pussy. The object, which seemed to have some kind of cold, jellied lubrication smeared over it intruded just beyond her nether lips.

Janice, expecting some kind of bizarre torture, began to wail and moan. She tried to shake off the device between her legs by moving her hips side to side, but it clung fast to her. There was a click and the pad that was nestled against her hooded clit began to vibrate. A tingle spread from her clit through her pussy. She shifted her hips anxiously. The probe between her nether lips was slowly urged forwards. Gradually, as Janice felt herself unwillingly stimulated by the vibrations against her clit, it slid forward until it was well seated within. Suddenly, the object, thick and now warm, began to vibrate and wriggle inside her. At the same time, the machine began to thrust it in and out of her now lubricated channel.

Janice could hear the giggles and the, no doubt, humorous comments of the Japanese girls above the mechanical whirring sound of the machine. She pulled and tugged at her bonds in protest at her treatment. But the faux penis that whirred and pulsed within her plush canal drove on relentlessly. The tingling in her loins grew to a kind of low burn, as the machine excited her against her will. Soon, her passions started to rise and the voices of the girls and the sounds of the machine began to fade away as her mind was drawn to the enflamed ember of lust within her.

On and on the machine went, dragging its hardness against her stiff clit, massaging the sides of her gushing slit. Janice, her mind momentarily refocused on her predicament and the humiliating circumstances of this assault on her sex, shook and ground her hips to expel the tantalizing intruder. But as her need for completion rose higher and higher, she let the darkness of her mask envelop her and block out all else but the pulsing in her loins.

Janice yearned to reach out and control the gyrating thrusts of the simulacrum within her. As with the Korean man who had assaulted her the day before, the girl was frantic that she was being driven to an unmanaged, unrestrained release of passion. She whined and moaned behind the gag, both in protest against her treatment and in almost agonizing pleasure as the relentless probing of her cunt threatened to push her over the edge.

When the telltale signs of her impending release came, Janice shook her body in protest, straining to free herself. She turned her face back and forth and screamed into the leather plug that filled her mouth. Her body shuddered as her pussy began to convulse. Jolt after jolt of exquisite pleasure flowed through her. Her hips thrust against her intruder, unwillingly seeking to drive the false prick deeper within her. "Ough! Ough! Ough! Ough!' she called out at each pulse of pleasure, her voice muffled by the cruel gag. She had never experienced anything like it. Just as she had feared, her body was unable to obey her mental commands to suppress the sinful sensations. "Ough! Ough! Ough!" she called out as her orgasm continued.

Finally, mercifully, her body began to calm. Her breathing was deep and labored. She could feel the sweat on her chest and her thighs. She expected the mechanical dildo to be withdrawn from her now that she had produced the obviously desired response. But, as the machine kept thrusting away, and the plastic intruder continued its dance within her, Janice realized that her tormentor was not to be satisfied with one orgasm. "Ooooohhhhhhh!" she moaned as she felt her pussy begin to tingle all over again.

As her lusts began to build anew, Janice wondered what strange world she had been drawn into. Had she been brought here to entertain the young Japanese girls whose exclamations of approval and merriment she could still hear? It seemed doubtful. But why was she being forced to make this obscene exhibition for them? Or was it for someone else? Were they just incidental to her main purpose here? Was someone else watching?

After her third, wrenching orgasm, Janice felt the machine being switched off. Her mask was removed. Her body was limp with expended passion. The matron uttered some sharp words in Japanese and the girls who had been watching tittered and left the room, dragging their secretarial chairs behind them. Her hands were released and the top to the table that she was on was lowered. The electrodes were removed from her chest.

The matron made some more entries in the clipboard and then urged Janice off of the table. When she stood up, her legs almost failed her as she was still experiencing the remnants of her long bout with the infernal machine. The exhausted girl stood docilely as the matron reattached her wrists behind her. She had a leash which she fastened to a ring in the front of the gag. Janice felt herself tugged forward.

She was led back out into the large room where the Japanese girls worked. They were busy at their phones and computers. The matron led the bound girl across the room to a small, steel elevator door. She pushed the button and the door opened. The ride up was long and fast. Janice had to steady herself as the acceleration of the elevator pressed down on her. There were only three buttons on the elevator for floors to exit on. The matron has pressed the topmost button. The elevator had only one possible destination, the penthouse floor.

When the elevator opened, Janice was surprised to see a large, smartly decorated room. It had a low ceiling, sporting small high-hat lights strewn around it. The lighting was soft, but still bright enough so that the room did not seem dark or sinister. A large abstract painting hung along one wall, blue swirls covered over by large squares of orange, green and red. The thick rug was soft on her bare feet. Janice could see out of the floor to ceiling length windows on one side of the room an unfamiliar urban landscape. She could be anywhere.

The matron towed Janice across the room to where a receptionist sat at a large desk. She was Asian, Japanese, Janice guessed, and older than the young women who had witnessed her orgasmic display. She was dressed in a conservative, corporate business style. Her desk was neat and clear, extending in a large 'L' around her. The desk defended a set of twin doors that extended from the floor to the ceiling. On each door was a large Japanese ideogram that looked like a wood carving. They were embossed in gold.

The black haired woman did not look up as Janice and the matron approached. Janice noted a set of larger elevators along another wall, presumably for use by those other than forlorn prisoners. The young girl looked back at the two large, ornate doors behind the secretary's desk. Somehow she sensed that behind that door she would learn the purpose of her coerced arrival at this strange place and what they wanted from her. She was not in a hurry to learn as she realized from all that had happened so far that it was probably not good. She felt her body trembling in fear. She fought back the tears that threatened to further embarrass and demean her. She wanted to be strong, to endure whatever these people had in store for her. Somehow, she knew she would escape.

The woman was on the telephone. She was speaking in almost perfect English to someone.

"No, Mr. Kuribashi cannot speak to you right now. He is in conference," she said in a stern, officious voice. "I will give him the message that you called." She listened for a moment. "Yes, I have your telephone number. Good bye."

As she placed the phone on the receiver, she looked up at Janice and the matron. Janice expected some kind of surprise from her, or at least a visible reaction that reflected the absurdity of her standing there before her, naked, gagged and bound. But she didn't show any reaction at all.

"Mr. Kuribashi is expecting you," she said to the matron. "Please wait while I buzz him." The secretary pushed a button on the telephone and a deep male voice responded in a short, harsh tone. The secretary replied in Japanese, apparently communicating their presence. "Hai!" she said after a moment. She looked up at Janice's escort. "You may proceed," she said.

Janice gave a small whine as the matron pulled her forward. She didn't want to go into that room. She wanted to run away, to hide. The matron, sensing Janice's reticence, yanked on the leash harshly. Her action rattled Janice's teeth. The abject girl followed docilely.

When the door opened, Janice and the matron entered a large, luxurious office. It was at least 30' by 30' and was paneled in a dark mahogany. The area near the door contained large, black, leather couches set against the near and left walls with a large marble coffee table in front of them. Large framed paintings were mounted on the walls which, at a quick glance, looked like original French impressionists. The rug was a rich, dark maroon and was deep piled. As in the reception area outside, the room was lit by small high hats set into the ceiling. Past the front area of the room, the floor was raised. On it sat several solid wooden chairs with dark red leather padding facing a large hand carved ebony desk. Behind the desk was a vast mural depicting a massive struggle between two Japanese armies, swords and spikes thrust into angry action, grim faces of struggling warriors standing out like demons.

Janice felt herself being tugged into the center of the room. On one of the couches sat an elegantly dressed, tall, lithe woman, with long black hair. She looked Eurasian, with oriental features and slightly rounded eyes. He face was delicate. She was holding a slim glass of white wine in her graceful right hand. Bright red, long fingernails were mounted at the tip of each finger and she wore a thick, gold rope-like bracelet on her left wrist. There was a long, braided gold chain around her neck. She was wearing a black sheath dress with a deep 'vee' neck' that was pushed up high on her well toned, luxurious thighs as she sat in the chair. Her legs were crossed and she was talking to a man sitting next to her on the other couch. Her pouty lips were painted the same bright red as her nails and she was licking them with her delicate pink tongue as she spoke to the man. The sides of her small, round breasts peeked out between the plunging neckline of the dress.

The man was definitely not Asian. He had short, grayish hair that lay flat on his head. It was slightly receded, announcing the man's mature age. He had a strong, Roman nose and chin. He was also holding a glass of wine, and he sloshed it around in the glass as he spoke to the woman. His legs were crossed as well and Janice could see the bottoms of his shiny, black shoes. He was wearing grey flannel trousers and a pastel blue shirt. His tie was knotted thickly at his neck, and was dark blue and covered with some kind of little russet designs.

Janice was humiliated to be standing naked in front of these sophisticated looking strangers. She suppressed her urge to whine as she was afraid that if she made any noise they would both look at her. She wanted to delay that moment as long as possible. She looked up at the desk on the platform. There was a large, black, leather chair behind the desk with its back towards the room. She could hear a man's voice speaking in gruff, deep Japanese.

The two women stood silently in the middle of the room for at least fifteen minutes. The matron had released the leash from Janice's collar and placed the clipboard on the marble table. From time to time, the woman or the man on the sofas would glance upwards and take in the naked form of the prisoner before them. But they would immediately return to their obviously entertaining conversation. They were speaking in Japanese but an occasional English word intruded. The woman laughed pleasantly at some joke that the man made. Janice could see the sexual interest in the woman's eyes each time that she looked at her. She was wearing red high heels and one dangled from the foot of the uppermost of her crossed legs.

Finally, the man behind the desk returned his telephone to the receiver. He spun around in his chair. He was a well muscled Japanese man with short, jet black hair. His face was broad and his nose flat. He had a sharp, almost upturned chin. His eyes floated over Janice, appraising her casually. He barked a command to the matron, who bowed, released Janice's chain and withdrew from the room.

As cruel as the matron had been to her, Janice bemoaned her departure. Somehow that absence of the hard, big boned woman made her feel more naked than before. Maybe it was because of the fact that the gruff Caucasian woman had at least seen her when she wasn't naked and bound, knew that she had some other existence than as an abject, naked spectacle.

The man sprung up from his chair and approached Janice, hopping athletically down the step into the lower area of the room. The man and the woman who had been chatting stood up. Janice wanted to run, but she had nowhere to go. She couldn't open the door with her hands bound behind her and there were three of them to her one, two of them well built, muscular men. She felt tears forming in her eyes as the Asian man, who she presumed to be Mr. Kuribashi, approached her. Her body recoiled and she tried to step back when he put his hands up to her breasts. He caught her nipples between the pointer finger and thumb of each hand and held the frightened woman fast. He spoke to the couple in Japanese.

"*What is this new employee's name?*" he asked.

The tall woman spoke. "*Her name is Janice, Kuribashisama,*" she said.

"Janeees?" the Asian man asked in confirmation.

"*Hai, Kuribashisama,*" the young woman replied.

"*Well, she's late,*" Kuribashi said accusingly. "*Whose responsibility was it to recruit her?*"

"*Genji Yashimura, Kuribashisama,*" the woman replied bowing slightly.

"*Please tell him that I am disappointed,*" he told the woman. "He must do better."

"*As you wish, sir,*" she answered.

Kuribashi had held tightly on to Janice's nipples during this brief exchange. Janice struggled to suppress a moan as the fingers pinched her painfully. His easy assumption of the right to manhandle her flesh, and his casual conversation with the other people in the room in his foreign tongue disconcerted her. The man turned and looked deeply into her face. His crisp, stern manner frightened her as did the deference to him of the other people in the room. They were both standing, awaiting Kuribashi's pleasure. The man released her nipples and cupped her breasts, weighing them in his hands, squeezing them gently.

"*Very nice,*" he said out loud to himself. His eyes watched hers as he massaged the heavy orbs. Janice's eyes, wide as saucers, stared back forlornly at the hard, muscular man. Janice fought off the urge to pull away. To her dismay, her sex began to tingle as a result of the heat of his hands on her breasts. Her eyes were glued to his, as if she were mesmerized. He smiled at her, enjoying her discomfort. She could feel the strength of his hard hands as they gently caressed her orbs, kneading them softly, covering her stiff nipples with his palms.

The Asian released Janice's breasts and, grabbing her shoulders, forced her to turn around. She shivered as he ran his hands down her shoulders and arms. He lifted her joined wrists with one hand and caressed the softness of her pale white rear globes. Janice quailed with fright as her vulnerability overwhelmed her. The man lifted her wrists higher, forcing her to bend forwards, straining her shoulders. She moaned with discomfort. Kuribashi measured her firm thighs with his free hand, issuing a satisfied grunt. Janice clamped her thighs tightly together, mortified that her delicate nether lips would be exposed to the callous view of the three strangers behind her. Kuribashi reared back his hand and gave her a mighty slap on her buttocks. The sound of the blow echoed through the room. The discomforted girl gave a sharp cry, muffled by her gag. Tears sprang to her eyes as the sharp pain coursed through her. Kuribashi issued a curt order in Japanese. His meaning was clear.

Reluctantly, tearfully, Janice spread her legs, giving the man access to her sex. She whined as she felt his hand pass over her mons, stroking it softly. His finger traced the length of her slit. Janice knew that he would find her moistened as the attention to her breasts and thighs had precipitated unwanted arousal. The finger slipped inside easily.

Kuribashi laughed. "*She's all wet!*" he said to the others as his finger entered Janice's moist tunnel. He removed it only to reenter, this time with three of his hard, fat fingers. Janice felt the walls of her pussy pushed aside as the man plunged his fingers back and forth within her. Her shoulders ached with the strain of her upraised wrists. She felt herself getting hot, her lust sparked by the man's unconsented to penetrations. Her breasts swayed gently below her chest in response to the pistoning of the man's hand. The room was silent, and she could hear her own labored breathing as her passion began to rise. She yearned to expel the torturous digits from within her, but, at the same time, her sex yearned for the ministrations of the man's hand to continue. To her regret and mortification, she moaned, unable to contain the product of the man's abuse of her flesh. Her thighs began to tremble as she felt her need build inside her. When she moaned again, she heard the Asian man laugh and he withdrew the tormenting fingers from her hot canal.

"*Excellent!*" he said to the others, smiling in satisfaction. "*But she has to be punished.*"

Janice cried with frustration as she felt he fingers leave her. The man released her wrists and, grabbing her hair, pulled her back upright. Janice heard the whirring of a small electric motor. She was spun around and saw a chain descending from the ceiling above her. The tall, lithesome woman stood behind her and unfastened her wrists only to bring them in front of her and attach them to the chain. The short haired Caucasian man was at the wall where he was operating a switch. When he pushed it, Janice felt her arms pulled up over her head. Her arms rose until her toes just brushed the floor.

The Eurasian woman had retrieved two leather belts from a side cabinet and kneeling down, fastened Janice's ankles and thighs together, pulling the belts tight around them. Janice could feel her wet pussy pressed tightly between her thighs, her moisture having leaked and wet the tender skin between them. She knew that something unpleasant was about to happen and she whined behind her gag in futile protest. The woman stood before her and, taking her leather encased chin in her hands addressed the unhappy girl.

"You have caused your employer much trouble by your disobedience," she said in lightly accented English. "You must be punished." The woman stood back and Janice saw that the Japanese man had a short, thick bamboo pole in his hand. He passed it to the tall, muscular Caucasian. He spoke to him in Japanese.

"*The ten pointed star,*" he instructed him.

The Caucasian man gave Kuribashi a small bow and approached the forlorn dangling woman. Janice was trying to convey her pleas for mercy through the thick leather plug in her mouth. She didn't mean to have been disobedient. She would do anything they wanted. She would do anything to avoid the fierce pain she knew that she was about to experience.

The Caucasian looked over Janice's helpless form as it dangled in front of him. She had delectable curves and an ample, inviting bosom. Her eyes were alight with fear. Her supplications to be spared her upcoming ordeal emerged as gentle mews from behind her gag. Lines of perspiration were snaking slowly down her sides and her body swayed gently as she struggled in her bonds.

The man looked at Kuribashi who had assumed a sitting position on the edge of the platform on which his desk sat. He had lit a cigarette and the blue grey smoke drifted lazily to the ceiling. He nodded at the other man. Janice, watching intently every move of the man before her, knew that that was the signal for her torment to begin. She uttered a long, desperate wail and steeled herself for the blow.

The bamboo pole had a leather handle on one end and the man gripped it tightly in his right hand. He walked slowly around the crying girl three times. He had seen Janice's body tense in anticipation of his attack and he was waiting for the tenseness of her body to lessen. She could not hold that pose indefinitely.

As Janice loosened her body so that she could take a deep breath of air, the man swung the pole swiftly and forcefully across the front of Janice's pretty, graceful thighs.

The blow sent an angry message of throbbing pain through the helpless and frantic young woman. She cried out in agonized pain, "Ahhhhhhhhhh!" She had barely recovered when the man delivered a second blow to the back of her thighs. "Ahhhhhhhhh!" she cried out again, her voice rendered almost mute by the thick leather gag in her mouth. She bit down on it in agony as she tried to cope with the insult to her flesh. She had clenched her eyes shut at the first blow, and when she opened them she could see the Asian man smiling appreciatively at her. The Eurasian woman had recovered her flute of white wine and was sitting next to him, her legs crossed, his hand around her waist. What strange, cruel world had she entered, she wondered fearfully as her legs throbbed with the dull residual of the man's assault.

He had circled again in front of her and he swung the bamboo pole once more, rearing back to gain the maximum momentum. It gave out a low 'whirrr" as it passed through the air and a loud "thump!" as it struck across her defenseless belly. Janice felt the breath knocked from her lungs from the force of the pole across her stomach.

"Ohhhhhhhhhhh!" she moaned as she struggled to draw in air to her lungs. Her body twisted and turned in anguished reaction to her torment.

It seemed to Janice that her torture would never end. Again and again the man laid the stiff, hard bamboo pole into her. He struck the back of her calves, the small of her back. Blows fell again on her thighs, this time on the outside of them, on her left and right. The seventh and eighth blows were applied to her ribs on each side of her, just underneath her outstretched arms. The ninth landed, agonizingly, across her defenseless breasts.

Janice did not know that the Asian man had prescribed that she suffer ten lashings in punishment of her disobedience. She was virtually mindless from the pain as she felt her legs loosened. Never had she experienced anything approximating the merciless assault on her body. She was swaying and moaning, praying that her ordeal be at an end. Her muscles throbbed and ached from the heavy blows. But the Caucasian man had struck her only nine times. There was one more to go. Janice felt one end of a strap fastened around her right ankle. Her legs were lifted high and the strap was threaded behind her shoulders and fastened to the other ankle. Her rear was raised high and her legs framed her neck. She was bent in two in a grotesquely obscene way. She looked up to see her sex prominently displayed between her thighs, the lips slightly parted. She saw the man pause before her. All at once, she realized what his next target would be. She cried and moaned in protest, begging him with her muffled voice to spare her body this painful insult.

The only sound in the room was Janice's anguished, muted protests. The Eurasian woman drained her glass and licked her lips in anticipation of this last, most painful assault. Kuribashi was staring at her fiercely, his lips drawn tight in an appreciative grimace. The Caucasian man stood next to the frightened young woman and drew his hand across her exposed pussy lips. He rubbed them gently, prying them apart with his fingers and teasing the nub of pleasure at their apex until they began to spread wide and engorge with blood.

Janice moaned and whined, hating her responsiveness to his efforts, her whole body still throbbing and aching from the blows of the bamboo pole. When his hand withdrew, Janice steeled herself for the assault on her puffy, moist sex. She whined and moaned, praying in her mind for deliverance from her surreal torment. She watched as the man raised the pole over his head. With a smile, he swung it forwards. It landed, as designed, square between the tender lips surrounding Janice's tender hole. When it landed, propelled with the full force of the gray haired man's right arm, Janice screamed with pain. It was if her whole being was centered on the point of contact between the hard, cruel pole and her sex. "Ahhhhhhrgh!" she cried, agony filling her whole being. Her strangely bound body swayed back and forth as the torment pulsed through her.

The three strangers waited patiently for Janice's mournful moaning to subside. In her mind, Janice struggled to deny the hard, cruel fate that had befallen her. "Please let it be over! Please! Please!" she cried out to herself.

Finally, her tormented body at rest, Janice felt her legs released and guided gently to the floor. Her face was awash with her tears, her eyes red rimmed.

The woman was holding a file in her hands, perusing it. "*She hasn't filled out her survey,*" she told the Asian executive. He just shook his head.

"*Two strokes,*" he responded with an exasperated tone.

The Eurasian woman stepped up to Janice and showed her the incomplete form. "You have been most uncooperative," she said in a lilting, almost sing-song accent. "Mr. Kuribashi has ordered that you be given two more strokes."

Janice's eyes lit up in terrorized fright. She ruefully regretted her lack of cooperation. If she could just talk! She would swear an oath on her own grave to obey! She would do anything they asked! Her desperate pleas were muffled by the thick wad of leather in her mouth. She pulled and tugged at her bonds, frantic to escape.

The European man, still holding the bamboo pole in his right hand smiled at the forlorn girl. Quicker than her eye could fathom, his hand darted out towards the poor girl. She felt, almost before she could see it, the pole strike across the tops of her breasts. She began to howl with pain. She danced and moaned as the insult to her flesh coursed through her. Before she had time to recover, the Caucasian man struck again, this time catching the breasts right across the nipples. Again, the wave of pain rushed through her. She slumped in her chains, unable even to stand. She hung her head and sobbed.

"*This one will take careful training,*" Kuribashi said.

The Caucasian man spoke up for the first time. "*She has great potential. And her body is a delight to torment.*"

The woman laughed. "*Hans has a one track mind, Kuribashisama.*"

"*Oh no, Yukio,*" the grey haired man retorted. "*Two tracks. In fact,*" he continued, "*if there's nothing else, I'm going to take her downstairs and fuck her.*"

It was Kuribashi's turn to laugh. "*Not before she takes care of me. She has raised my pole, now she must salute it.*"

All three of them laughed. Their mirth was not shared by Janice who, besides being ignorant of the nature of the discussion around her, was too beaten and forlorn to follow much of anything. She did notice it when the woman released her hands from over her head. The gray haired man held her, preventing her from falling to the floor while the Eurasian woman refastened her hands behind her back. When the naked girl had steadied, Hans pulled her forward by the ring in her collar. He put his hands on her shoulders until she began to sink to her knees. Her gaze had been downcast, but when she sensed the figure of the man the woman called Kuribashi in front of her, she looked up. He was seated on the edge of the platform leading up to the desk area of the room. His fly was open and his rock hard cock was standing up from it. Janice gave a little whine.

She felt the gag released from behind her head and the thick, leather plug withdrawn from her mouth. She wanted to beg the people to let her go, to free her. She wanted to explain that it was some kind of mistake, that she didn't want to be here. But she remained silent. The woman spoke to her again. "You must pleasure Mr. Kuribashi now," she said.

Janice nodded and, tearfully leaned over until her face was in Kuribashi's lap. Timidly, she parted her lips and surrounded the bulbous head of his cock. Despair swept over her as she realized that all of her will had been taken away from her. She had been here, wherever here was, for less than half a day and already she had surrendered all that she was to the command of these cruel people. Her stomach fluttered as she tasted the salty flesh of Kuribashi's meat on her lips. With a bitter sob, she pressed her head down-wards.

The hot meat filled her mouth. She ran her lips down the shaft sucking gently, afraid to cause the man any discomfort. She trembled in fear and humiliation as she rode the tool with her mouth. What she had only done privately, and on her own terms, she now was doing in full view of the man and woman behind her, perfect strangers. She had used her oral skills to obtain power over her sometimes obnoxious and demanding boyfriends. If they wanted this, they had to be nice to her. But now, she felt no sense of power, even as she heard the Japanese man moan with pleasure. All of the power flowed from him. She felt his stiff, hard power in her mouth as she danced her tongue around it, squeezed it tightly with her lips. She felt his powerful hands on her head as he encouraged her movements up and down. It was as if her whole existence centered around the rock hard pole.

Yukio and Hans admired Janice's sleek back, bent over to her task, and her plump, but graceful, rear cheeks. Her hands were clenched tightly behind her back as her body protested its abasement. Her long, auburn hair hung down over her shoulders, draping her face.

Janice prayed for her ordeal to end as she used all her able efforts to bring the Japanese man off. He had used his hands to slow her pace, luxuriating in the oral caress of his manhood. Suddenly, his muscles tensed and he groaned loudly. A fist grabbed Janice's hair behind her head and started to pump it furiously on his cock. Janice was taken aback by her callous use and whined with dismay. And then she felt the cock spasm within her and a jet of hot cum splash against the back of her mouth. Kuribashi gave a loud shout, startling her. She swallowed his viscous load without hesitation, something she had never done for anyone. She knew without being told that reticence would not be tolerated. Besides, what if some got on his $2,000 dollar suit? He would whip her until she bled.

Janice felt her stomach revolt against the bitter and salty taste of her employer's spunk. But when the throbbing of his organ in her mouth subsided, she was relieved. His fist was still in her hair, but he had slowed the pumping of her head. Finally he released it, just as the softened appendage was about to slip from her lips of its own accord. He unhanded her hair and she felt two sets of hands pulling her to her feet. She was pulled back. A small drop of his come was hanging onto her lower lip and Yukio plucked it off with her finger. She presented it to Janice. "Lick my finger," she instructed the girl. Janice obediently and dismally obeyed.

Kuribashi had closed his pants and was standing again. "You must bow to Mr. Kuribashi and say thank you to him. Say '*Arigatou gozaimasu, Kuribashisama*,'" she told the girl slowly so she could catch the unfamiliar phrase. Janice hesitated. She was supposed to thank him! She grimaced sourly at the macabre supposition that she should be grateful for having her mouth raped by this terrible man. But she remembered the bamboo pole and the whipping of her breasts. Clearly the world had developed new rules and she must follow them.

"*Agrigato…*," she stammered hesitantly, her voice low, timid.

"No," the woman said. "Repeat after me. '*Arigatou*'."

"*Arigatou*," Janice repeated.

"*Gozamasu*."

"*Gozamasu*."

"*Kuribashisama.*"

"*Kuribashisama.*"

"Now bow and say it to Mr. Kuribashi."

Janice bent her frame forward. Her heart felt like lead and her whole body was shaking. The implications of this simple act of obeisance revolted her. But she did it. "*Arigatou gozamasu, Kuribashisama,*" she said miserably, her voice just above a whisper.

"*Dou itashi mashite,*" the man replied with a slight bow of his head. "Don't mention it."

Janice felt her head pulled back and the gag was reintroduced to her mouth. She groaned bitterly as she felt it jammed inside. The woman buckled it behind her head. She saw the gray haired man's hand reach below her chin and reattach the leash to her collar. Apparently, her introduction to the boss was over. She turned and saw a look of undisguised lust in the gray haired man's face. She shuddered at the implication. The man, her leash held firmly in his left hand, bowed to Mr. Kuribashi. He thanked the sturdy Asian for his hospitality. "*Osewa ni nari mahsita,*" he said. Kuribashi grunted in reply and acknowledged the bow with a slight one of his own. Janice felt her leash tugged to the side. The well built gray haired man strode purposely from the room. Janice, naked, bound and gagged, propelled by his firm hand on her leather leash, scurried after him.

勢覇

CHAPTER FIVE
ORIENTATION

When the well dressed, grey haired man dragged her from Kuribashi's office, he took her back to the elevator that she had come up in. She saw herself reflected in the gleaming polished steel of the elevator door while they waited for it to arrive. What she saw was a woman who had been totally transformed from free, liberated, outspoken and adventurous, to silent, ashamed, compliant and degraded. Her eyes met those of her possessor in the mirror like surface. They were as hard and as cold as the elevator door. He grinned at her and tightened his grip on her leash.

The doors slid open end Janice was pulled inside. She watched as the man hit the middle of the elevator's only three buttons. The elevator descended rapidly and then slowed to a stop. As her body tried to acclimate itself to the controlled fall, Janice felt the queasiness in her stomach that, as a young girl, she used to think was fun. Her knees bent slightly as the elevator smoothed to a stop. The steel door opened and the man propelled her into the narrow, dimly lit corridor outside.

The soft lighting of the narrow corridor created a dreamlike atmosphere. It was lit by small sconces located along the smooth, bare, brownish yellow walls. The floor was covered by a soft, deeply piled, brown rug. Janice followed the grey haired man along the small hallway, dragged along by the force of the leash connected to her collar. They passed several doors, all with large, ominous locks. After traveling about fifty feet, the corridor took a sharp turn to the left. The hallway stretched at least another fifty feet ahead before it made another leftward turn. The doors along this wall were numbered in both Arabic and ideographic numerals. There was a light fixture above each one, buried into the wall. Some of the lights were on and some off, the significance of which would occur to Janice later. The man halted outside of a door marked "4". There was a small disk hanging on a hook on the door with the same number. The light over the door was off. Hans, her captor, took the disk off of the hook and, releasing Janice's leash, clipped it to the ring on the frightened girl's collar. He looked at her with his steely gray eyes and spoke crisply to her. "Number four," he said. Janice tried to comprehend what he was saying to her. Was this her new name? Was he renaming her? "No!" her mind shouted. "My name is Janice! Janice Paterson! I am not a number!"

The well muscled but compact man turned to open the door in front of them. She could see his fingers dancing quickly over a combination lock. When there was a click and a green light appeared, the man put his hand in the pocket of his finely tailored suit jacket and produced a small plastic card.

Janice's leash hung free as the man swiped the card through a slot on the lock. There was a click and the lock popped open. The unhappy girl dreaded whatever was behind that door. It bode her no good. Once inside, she would be trapped, locked away, isolated, helpless. She turned to look down the corridor. Should she run? But to where? If she got to the elevator, she had no way to press its button to summon the car. She could run the other way, but had no reason to believe that freedom ran along that route. What chance did a naked, bound and gagged woman have anyway? She had been beaten unmercifully already. She did not want to give such obvious cause for punishment again. Tearfully, passively, she waited for the door to be opened.

When the door swung free, the man stepped back and, with a wave of his hand, invited the trembling girl to enter. A whine escaped from behind her thick leather gag, and she bit down on it harshly. Her bound arms writhed behind her as her body resisted obedience to the man's compulsory invitation. She had broken out in a light sweat and perspiration made her underarms and inner thighs slick. A knot had formed in her stomach and a sense of impending doom came over her. She knew that stepping through the doorway would confirm her status as an abject prisoner. Just as she had entered the limousine and been whisked away to this unknown location by her enforced consent, she would be entering this new form of hell by her own volition, under her own power, as if launching herself over a stark precipice, causing her body to tumble down into an unknown, fearful fate. All of her wanted to flee, to resist. But she knew that she had no choice. She had ceased having a choice about anything once she had made that fateful phone call three days ago. Since then, her fate had been sealed. Resistance now only put off and probably worsened the inevitable.

Her naked breasts swaying, her nipples stiff with fear, Janice forced her right leg forward, followed quickly by her left. She entered the room with the hard, cruel Caucasian man behind her. She heard the door close and lock in place.

There were no windows in the small room, and the lighting was as dim as in the hallway. She could feel a cool pad under her feet and saw, ominously, a small, steel cage set in the corner of the room. A futon was rolled up against the wall on her right with a small chest next to it. There was also what appeared to be a bottle of water and a lidded, porcelain pot. A wooden cabinet, stained a deep oak, was mounted into the wall. The room contained nothing else. In large, black strokes that ran the length of each side wall were the ideograms she had seen on Kuribashi's door. They dominated the room like two unfathomable monsters, their strange, intricate lines defying Janice's understanding.

Janice felt the man's hands unlock the leather cuffs behind her back and loosen the offensive leather gag whose shield had covered the lower half of her face. A pair of strong hands set on her shoulders and she turned as they forced her body around. The man removed the leash and tossed it to the corner of the room.

"Put you hands on your head," the man ordered in a quiet but curt tone. Janice complied dutifully. She had not studied the man's face closely before, and took the opportunity to examine it in the room's dim light. He was at least a foot taller than her and was standing no more than six inches from her face. She could see the ravaged muscles of his rough, pock marked cheeks, the fierce glare of his eyes. His nose was thick and long and his lips were thin. There was a small scar just under his left eye. His chin was square and well defined. Janice had never been this close to such a hard, cruel looking man, never mind being in his complete power. There was a heavy lump in her stomach as she realized that she was finally facing what she had feared the most. This man was going to rape her.

"Turn around," the man ordered, his words emerging slowly and with implied menace. He grinned evilly as he spoke. Janice, terrified of this man who had already cruelly abused her, turned slowly so that her back was again facing him. She could feel her hot blood rushing through her veins and the solid, frantic pumping of her heart. She had never been so afraid.

"Spread your legs," the man ordered harshly. Janice moved them apart obediently. Her eyes pinned to the vacant wall before her, the one opposite the door, where the window should have been, she heard the man move behind her. She heard the unmistakable sound of cloth sliding over cloth. Undoubtedly, the man was undressing in preparation of his assault on her.

Hans folded his clothes neatly on the floor. When he was completely naked, he advanced on the shivering girl before him. He took a moment to enjoy the pleasing curve to her hips, the plump, graceful form of her rear. He stepped up to her and placed his body against hers.

Janice jumped slightly as she felt the man's flesh pressed against her. It was hot and hard. His long, stiff cock nestled in the crack of her behind. Unwillingly, her pussy began to tingle in anticipation of its use. Hot, hard hands moved over her hips, across her stomach and seized her firm, taut breasts. She trembled with incipient passion as she felt the man's fingers pinch her distended nipples. Goose bumps rose all over her body. She uttered a quiet whine.

"What lovely breasts you have, Number Four," the man said, whispering into her ear. She could feel the man's hot breath and it produced a rush of cold fear that passed right through her.

"Oh, god, no," Janice pleaded silently. "Please don't let this happen, please, please!" She yearned to remove her hands from her head, to turn and defend herself and she cursed herself for her cowardice in failing to do so. The man's hands were like swarming leaches, covering her torso with their devilish touch. But Janice knew that she was faced with the inevitable. Alone, ensconced in a secret room on an unknown floor of an anonymous building, there would be no avoidance of her fate. She moaned as the man's right hand slid down over her firm, flat belly and mixed with the wiry hair that surmounted her lower lips. The hand probed her and she felt a finger trace the outline of her slit, finding it moist and receptive. "Ohhhhhhh!" she moaned, partly from her rising lust and partly from shame. She tried to will her body to resist the heat of her assailant's, to push back the warmth that was spreading through her loins. She bit her lip in frustrated agony.

Janice had fucked strange men before. A couple times out with the girls she had allowed herself to be picked up and taken to their apartments for a night of passion. But she had always made sure that she was firmly in control, made the men wait for her, coyly pushing away a hand, closing her legs to delay the man's satisfaction. She wanted them so hot that they would do anything she said, play by her rules. It was risky, but Janice was sure of herself and only picked the men that she knew she could handle.

But now, she was utterly without control. She could no more brush away the hand that was teasing her hardened clit than spit out diamonds. Her pussy lips still ached from their abuse with the whip. The door was locked and she was no match for this cruel, hard man who was possessing her.

His fingers had pried her pussy lips wide open and she felt him push them past the entrance, into her moist, hot channel. His other hand maintained the torment to her breasts, pinching and pulling at her teats, massaging their bulk. The girl moaned again and she felt her knees weaken. Lust was beginning to overcome her.

Suddenly, the man stepped back. "Open the futon," he ordered her sharply. Startled, Janice took her hands from the top of her head and sprang towards the wall. Hurriedly, lest she be punished for delay, she rolled the thick, soft mattress out. It was covered by a silk fitted sheet of delicate yellow. Two large, firm pillows sprung out as the futon was laid flat. It was as large as a queen sized bed, at least four inches thick. Its head was against the wall and it lay lengthways across the room.

"Lie down," the man spat out at the trembling girl. "On your back."

Janice looked up at the man's strange visage timidly as she first sank to her knees and then rolled over onto her back. The man looked down at her with obvious lust. His cock was rampant with his desire. Janice's stomach fluttered as she realized that in a moment that hard sword of flesh would pierce her. Her eyes grew wet with tears.

Still towering over her, the man commanded her to raise her knees, grab her ankles and pull her legs wide apart. As she did so, Janice realized that her bushy folds were exposed to the man's vision and his depredations. He knelt down between her knees and ran his hot hands over her inner thighs. He leaned forward over her, supporting himself with his left hand. His other hand had grabbed hold of his stiff rod and he pressed its tip against the entrance to Janice's molten cleft. He watched her lustful reaction as he slid its helmet along the length of her slit. "Ohhhhhhhh!," the girl moaned, her body twisting and turning beneath him. Her eyes had been closed, jammed tight, in a futile attempt to blot out the fact of her ravishment. But, at the sensation of the thick meat pushing her swollen nether lips apart, entering her, filling her needy, welcoming canal, she opened them and saw the harsh smile of her oppressor, his gleaming, amused eyes. Her stomach heaved in protest against her debasement. And then the steel hard cock slid home, the man's belly pressed up against hers and she sighed in a passionate misery.

As the fleshy pole slowly rasped along the length of her steamy sheath, Janice felt her need rushing higher and higher. The man was in no hurry and his deliberate, languorous strokes tortured her. Her mind longed to expel the relentless invader while her body welcomed each long, deep thrust.

The man had his hands on the mattress on either side of her and his contact with her body was limited to the interface of his long, thick rod and Janice's aching channel. Her hair was spread in a corolla around her head. She could hear the man's lustful, labored breaths as he reveled in her body. Her heart was thumping loudly in her chest and her passion was mounting. She wanted the man to end his torment of her. She closed her eyes and prayed for it to end just as her pussy's throbbing began. Suddenly, wave after wave of almost painful pleasure began to shoot through her. "Ohhhhhhh!" she moaned "Oh, god! Oh! Oh! Ohhhhh-hhhh!" she called out as her orgasm overcame her. Her thighs trembled and her body shook. Her breasts were heavy and full, the tips sharp and hard. "Ohhhhhhhh! she moaned again as the merciless cock drove her lust onwards.

Janice thought that she would not stop coming. The prick that impaled her kept up its remorseless pace. Just as she thought that her passion was spent, she felt it begin to rise again.

"Ohhhhh, please," Janice called out mournfully. She had no power to prevent her flesh from responding to the man's hot cock. As her body began to shiver and throb once more, she dug her heels deep into the mattress, grabbing her ankles ever more tightly. She yearned to release them to at least attempt to push her tormentor away, to protest the callous rape of her body. But she dared not. She had no courage to oppose this harsh, hardened man's will.

Janice began to cry even as her cunt spasmed with pleasure. The man began to thrust harder and she heard him grunt with passion. He took her head in his hands and pressed his lips to hers. His hands pried her jaws apart and his hot tongue forced it way into her mouth. "Mmmmmmmmmmmm!" Janice moaned in lust and protest. Her thighs clamped tightly against the man's hips. She felt her pelvis pushing back at the man's thrusts, needing him deep inside her, wanting his hot discharge to fill her.

"Argh! Argh! Argh!" the man called out as he pumped his semen deep into her womb, his hips slamming hard against hers. The sensation of the man's tensing body and the pulsing of his thick meat set Janice off once again and she writhed and rocked beneath him.

Janice had never come like this before. She had never wanted to. She feared the very passions that the strange man had released. As her wrenching spasms finally abated, she cried and cried. What had this man unleashed in her? What was she becoming? What did these people want from her?

Janice closed her eyes again as the shame of her lustful performance swept through her. She felt the man rise up from atop her and his turgid cock slide out from her burning pussy. She moaned as the man's weapon left her, the sensation of her now empty cunt overwhelming her.

The man rose to his feet and stepped to the wall. He grabbed the bottle of water that was there and took a long pull.

"Not bad, Number Four," the man said to her, his voice low and satisfied. "But you have a lot to learn. Now get up."

Reluctantly, slowly, her mind protesting her debasement, Janice rose from the soft, comfortable futon. "Roll it up," the man ordered coldly.

Janice obediently rolled the wide, fluffy mattress up against the wall. She could feel the man's eyes burning into her back as she bent over at her task. "What is next?" she wondered fearfully. "What will he do to me now?"

"Stand up. Hands on your head and turn around," the man ordered. As Janice obeyed and faced the far wall, she heard the man lift his clothes from the floor and begin to dress. She stood there silently, her arms aloft, elbows out, as he finished. She could feel the remnants of his discharge leaking down her thighs. Silently, he gathered her arms behind her back and clipped her wrists back together. The man reached around her front and pushed the thick leather gag between her teeth, buckling it behind her head. Janice cringed as she felt her mouth fill once more with the offensive mass. She tried desperately to hold back her tears as she felt a wave of self pity envelope her. "Why? Why? Why?' she cried out mentally to no one. "What is going to happen to me?"

The man walked in front of Janice and opened the door to the small steel cage that sat in the corner. "Get in," he said matter-of-factly. Janice looked at him forlornly. Hadn't she done what he asked? Hadn't she been obedient? Why did she have to be locked up?

As Janice's eyes begged the man's mercy, he stood there staring at her coldly. "I don't like to give orders twice," he said threateningly. "Now, get down on your knees and get in the cage."

With a piteous whine, Janice lowered herself to her knees. She crept over to the cage and, after a moment's frantic hesitation, pushed her body in. First her head, then her shoulders, and then, crunching her body in half, pulled in her thighs and feet. Her knees slid across the padded bottom. The steel of the cage pressed against her skin all around. Her head was bent and it took some effort to turn it so that she could see the legs and feet of the man standing behind her. She heard a cold, sharp click as the door to the cage was closed and the lock set.

The man bowed slightly to the imprisoned woman. "*Arigatou gozaimasu,*" he said politely. He turned and, unlocking the door, exited the room. He shut the light as he left.

For a brief moment, Janice held the image of the tiny room in her eyes. Then there was darkness, total and complete. It took about ten minutes for the full weight of her pitiful state to sink in. She was a prisoner in a tiny box in a dark and locked room far removed from anyone who would help or have mercy on her. Her mouth and her sex had been violated; she was deprived of her voice and the use of her hands. She had been beaten.

Janice began to sob uncontrollably. Her chest heaved with disconsolation. She screamed in rage and frustration, her voice emerging as a muffled whine. She banged her body against the bars of the cage fruitlessly. She yanked and pulled at her bound wrists and bit down harshly on the cruel wad of leather in her mouth. "No! No! No!" she screamed to herself. This could not be happening! This could not be real! Who were these people? Would she ever be free?

Realizing the futility of her revolt, Janice soon calmed herself. "I'll escape!" she thought. "There must be some way." But to where? She had learned already the power and reach of the organization that had imprisoned her. Why would it be any different the next time?

* * * * * * * * * * *

It seemed like hours that Janice was confined in the inky darkness. She heard nary a sound other than her own breathing. Her leg muscles and back were beginning to ache miserably. When the light went back on, Janice expected someone to come into the room. But she was wrong. Many minutes passed, an hour, maybe two, before there was any movement at the door. Janice took the time to examine her prison in detail. She saw the ominous hooks in the ceiling and walls, undoubtedly designed to facilitate her torture. Several switches were set into the far wall and, next to the door, which sat on the far right side of the room, was what appeared to be the eye of a camera. Under it were a series of small lights.

Being able to see the rest of the room from the confines of her tiny cage, made her imprisonment there seem all the more strange and abject. She stared at the rolled up futon, the stage on which her recent debasement had taken place. How soon would her back be again laid across it while the grey haired man or someone else ploughed her disobedient furrow? She recalled her lustful responses shamefully. Were they right in forcing her to service them? Had they discovered her heretofore unknown, subterranean nature, her secret wantonness?

Finally, the door opened. Janice had drifted of into a half sleep and she was, for a moment, disoriented and confused as to where she was. But it was only for a moment, and the all too real nature of her plight drove a spike through her heart.

It was a middle aged Asian woman who had entered, dressed in a dark green kimono, with wooden sandals on her feet. She had long, black hair streaked with grey that was gathered at the back of her head in a bob. She had long, boney fingers and wrinkled hands.

The woman looked at Janice for a long time, seemingly appraising her. Janice prayed that she would release her from her tiny cage. She would do anything to get out. She looked at the woman pleadingly.

After a few moments, the woman advanced across the room and Janice heard the lock to her cage undone. The woman barked a sharp command to her in a foreign tongue which Janice took, correctly, to be an order to remove herself from the cage. She shimmied herself out and proceeded to a spot in the middle of the room at which the older lady pointed. The woman went to the wall and lifted the porcelain bowl and brought it to Janice. She removed its lid and uttered another sharp command to the bewildered and naked girl. Janice stared back uncomprehendingly. The woman shook her head as if commenting on the stupidity of her charge. She lifted the edge of her kimono with both hands and squatted over the bowl. Janice heard the unmistakable sound of a jet of urine being splashed against the bowl's bottom. The woman's eyes bore into Janice's as she emptied her bladder. When done, she removed a tissue from her pocket and wiped herself clean. Throwing the tissue in the bowl, she rose and repeated her prior command to Janice.

The girl found it difficult to maintain her balance over the commode with her hands fastened behind her back, but she was just able to squat astride the urinal. It took a few moments for her to summon up her flow, but, despite her chagrin and embarrassment, was able to let her liquids go. Her bladder had been aching with need for a long time and she was actually grateful for the opportunity to empty it. The Asian woman smiled condescendingly as if appreciating the learning of a trick by a pet. When Janice was finished, the woman removed another tissue from her pocket and wiped the young girl clean. She then motioned the girl to resume her knees and, after lidding the pot, placed it back against the wall.

She picked up the water bottle and brought it to where Janice knelt. Placing it on the floor before her, the woman reached behind Janice's head and unbuckled her gag. She removed the wad of leather from Janice's mouth and, picking up the bottle of water, gave the poor girl to drink.

Janice hadn't realized how thirsty she was until the cool liquid began to flow down her throat. It was like heaven, and the refreshing feeling she got from its consumption caused her hopes to rise. "I can survive this," she thought. "I can. I can."

Maybe this woman would help her, Janice thought. When the bottle was removed from her mouth and the last gulp receded down her throat, Janice whispered a quiet plea to the woman. "Please help me," she said quietly. "Please let me out. Please."

The Asian woman looked at Janice as if she had just shat on her shoe. She reached into the pocket of her kimono and removed a silver pen like instrument. Janice recognized it at once. It was the same as the nurse had carried. As the Asian woman snapped it open, Janice realized her dreadful mistake.

Frantically, the young woman tried to scramble away. "No! Please don't hit me! Please!" she yelled. She felt the fire-like sting of the whip against her flesh. "Owwwwwww!" she cried out. Silently, the Asian woman followed the terrified girl around the room, striking unmercifully her thighs, back, buttocks and her bound arms with the steel whip. "Ohhhhh! Ohhhhhhh!" Janice cried out. "Please, please, I'll be good! Please!"

Finally the woman ceased her pursuit. Janice was huddled in a corner trembling and crying. She looked up at the woman forlornly. The woman pointed to a spot in the middle of the room with the whip. Reluctantly, fearful of additional torment, Janice crawled to that spot. She knelt there in fear, trembling as the Asian woman glared down at her. "No talk!" she yelled at the girl. "*Shizukani!*" she shouted as if the order to remain silent was more binding if expressed in Japanese. Janice nodded sheepishly. Her skin burned from the lashes and tears flowed down her cheeks. When the Asian woman proffered the dreaded gag to her mouth, Janice meekly accepted it.

The woman retrieved Janice's leash from the floor and, after attaching it to her collar, pulled her to her feet. She dragged her to the door and, unlocking it, led her into the hallway. She followed the diminutive, slightly bent woman as she headed down the hall. As they went, she was surprised and shocked to see another naked young woman, her hands bound behind her, her mouth gagged, standing by another door while a heavy set Asian man was unlocking it. Their eyes met momentarily and Janice saw the look of resignation in the girl's expression. She had short, blond hair cut close to her head. She bore the marks of the whip across her snow white skin. Janice slowed as she neared the woman, amazed that her fate was shared. The blond woman turned her eyes away just as Janice was passing her and the Asian woman yanked at Janice's leash to force her to resume her pace. As she went further down the corridor, Janice heard the door behind her close.

Janice's voyage through the dimly lit hallway continued for some time. Finally, the Asian woman stopped at a door and opened it. The room was small and dim just like Janice's cell. She brought Janice to the center of the room and pushed her to her knees. There was a short steel pole embedded in the floor and the woman affixed the front of Janice's collar to the top of it. She took a long, leather thong from the wall and tied it around Janice's right knee. She then passed it around the pole, winding it around it twice and circled Janice's other knee with it. The result left Janice kneeling and unable to rise or to turn her body. The woman went to the wall in front of Janice and opened a panel behind which was a large TV screen. She fiddled with the dials and the screen came to life. The woman left the room.

At first, there were only the strange ideograms that Janice had seen on the door to Mr. Kuribashi's office when she first arrived and which were imprinted upon her prison cell's walls. They were a bright, angry red set on a black background. Then there was a swelling of orchestral music and then a picture of a large office building situate in some kind of huge park. It was an aerial shot and the camera zoomed up, over and around the building until it was ground level and looking up at a great sign in Japanese ideograms and in English. It read 'The Budikan Corporation'. A pleasant, slightly accented woman's voice came on.

"Greetings from the corporate management of the Budikan Corporation and congratulations on your selection as a corporate comfort girl. You will have many questions about your new responsibilities. This orientation message will answer many of them."

(The camera shifts to a view of several pretty, young, occidental women dressed in kimonos, smiling and bowing to the camera.)

"First of all, you should be assured that the Budikan Corporation is committed to providing you all the necessities of life. You will no longer have to worry about medical care, housing, clothing or food, as these will all be provided to you. But, in your new position as a corporate comfort girl, you will have many responsibilities in return."

(The camera shifts again to a picture of a naked woman bowing lowly before a well dressed Asian man. The man is smiling appreciatively.)

"It will be your duty to bring physical pleasure to the valued customers, associates, friends and fellow employees of the Budikan Corporation. You have been chosen because you have been deemed appropriately quailfied for this position."

(The scene now is of several young women, kneeling in a circle, their hands atop their heads. They are naked and all wear the same collars and bracelets as Janice.

They are gagged and they all look up forlornly at the camera as it pans around them)

"For the next several weeks, you will undergo a rigorous training. This is to instill in you a dedicated commitment to your new position as well as to impress upon you the need for absolute obedience to your superiors and to the valued friends of the Corporation that you will be detailed to serve. You are now part of the Budikan family and are expected to devote yourself wholly to your responsibilities."

(The screen now shows a raven haired, young woman naked and on her knees. Her mouth encircles a stiffened cock belonging to a man whose naked body is seen only from the waist down. The woman's lips are assiduously working the man's rod while her hands cup his swollen sac beneath. Her eyes are open wide and looking up lovingly at the man whom she is servicing. The camera lingers on her dedicated efforts for about thirty seconds before the voiceover resumes.)

"You will learn to take pleasure and pride in your ability to provide bodily comfort and enjoyment to others."

(The next scene shows a pale skinned woman with long, blond hair. Her hands are raised above her head and attached to a ring in a post. She wears a leather shield across the lower half of her face. A man stands before her, his back to the camera. It is peering over his shoulder at the unhappy looking girl. He is also naked and he holds in his right hand a long, leather switch. He rears back and strikes the woman across her breasts. The woman screams and moans behind her gag and a bright red line appears.)

"Incorrect behavior or failure to devote yourself enthusiastically to your tasks will be severely punished."

(The man continues whipping the girl and she continues to scream and moan as she dances furiously in place.)

"Furthermore, you must provide pleasure to those assigned to you regardless of what form of pleasure they desire. From time to time, a guest or associate may wish to derive enjoyment from your suffering. You will learn to submit to such suffering obediently, with the happy thought that you are serving the best interests of the Budikan Corporation."

(The camera returns to the large office building in the first shot. It draws back and the building becomes rendered in a drawing form and begins to shrink. The camera keeps withdrawing until it shows a globe of the earth. The globe begins to spin and little flags with the red ideogram on a black background that was first shown in the beginning of the program begin to appear on it, strewn haphazardly over all of the continents.)

"The Budikan Corporation has facilities worldwide and is a very large company with varied interests. You can take pride that you will be contributing your part to make the company's projects a success."

(The scene shifted back to the happy women dressed in kimonos. They were still smiling and were now bowing obsequiously to the camera.)

"Rejoice in your good fortune in having become a part of such an important and worthwhile endeavor. Good bye and *guddorakku!* Good luck!" (Fade to black.)

Janice was stupefied. She could hardly believe what she had just heard. She was a 'comfort girl'? Her mind revolted at the thought. She anxiously tugged at the bonds that held her wrists while she pulled her neck back, straining her linkage to the short post in front of her. She bit down on her gag and moaned loudly. "Nooooooooo!" she wailed. "Please no!" She screamed inwardly. "Oh, god, this must be some kind of horrible dream! It can't be real!"

All of this pretense about corporate employment didn't fool her. She had been recruited as a slave, a sexual slave. Her body would be polluted by all kinds of men, all using her under a polite fiction that she was some kind of hospitality hostess. She had never heard of the Budikan Corporation, but it sounded powerful. When they had finished 'training' her, would she be sent to one of the corporation's remote outposts? Would she ever see her family again, she wondered unhappily. Would she ever be a free woman again?

The television in front of Janice began to whir and the disc or tape or whatever it was started all over again. Janice stared at the bright red logo with hatred and fear. She was the property of this corporation. They had stolen her and were going to turn her into a whore.

There seemed to be no hurry to advance Janice to the next stage of her debasement. The video stopped playing after the third showing and the distraught young woman knelt in place for a long time before the door opened again. All the time, the screen had been filled with the dreaded logo of the Budikan Corporation. It was burned into Janice's mind like a mental tattoo. Its strange and unfamiliar shape seemed demonic to her. The ideograms demanded obedience from her, declared her worthless except in how she could serve it. It shone out remorselessly from the screen.

It was the same salt and pepper haired woman who came for Janice. She undid the girl's knees and then unhooked her collar from the short pole. Once the leash was reattached, she led her out the door and further down the hall.

This time, they did not encounter anyone else. Janice wondered how many women were here in 'training' as they had put it. Where did they come from? Had they been recruited like she was, betrayed by a letter from a friend? The highest number she had seen on any of the doors had been '10'. A couple of the doors with the large Arabic and Japanese numbers still had a small disk hooked outside them, presumably for girls who had not yet been 'recruited'.

The woman stopped by another door and knocked. A buzzer sounded and the door sprung open. The woman towed her unhappy prisoner in. The small room was an anteroom for another office. A young Japanese woman sat at a desk. She was typing on her computer. The matron bowed lowly to her and said something in Japanese. The young woman gave a curt reply and the matron brought Janice over to the wall to the secretary's right. She connected the leash to a hook on the wall, turned, bowed to the secretary again and left.

Janice was appalled to be left standing there, naked and bound before the pretty, young secretary. Since her mouth was gagged, she couldn't ask what she was doing here. The secretary, Janice thought, was certainly more pretty than her. Why wasn't she recruited as a 'comfort girl'? It wasn't fair. She didn't want to be a whore. She gave out a small whine as her despair enwrapped her heart.

The Japanese girl looked up when she heard the involuntary sound that Janice had made. She saw that the attractive, young woman (Janice wasn't really fair to herself; she was, in fact, quite appealing) was staring at her, a forlorn look in her eyes. She seemed annoyed. "You must maintain silence, Number Four," she said in a brisk manner. "And don't look at me. It's annoying."

A tear ran down from Janice's left eye as she received the instructions of the other young woman. Something in Janice refused to believe that the young woman could really have so cold a heart not to take pity on her. She tried to make contact.

"Eeeeeese, eeeeeeeese," she managed to sound through her gag. "Elllll eeeeeee, eeeeese!" The gag retarded Janice's ability to make hard consonant sounds and that was about as close as she could get to an abject plea for help. The secretary looked up at Janice with a disdainful, disgusted look. Janice watched her as she got up from the desk. She opened a drawer and took something out. "Maybe it's the key to the locks," Janice thought hopefully.

But when the girl came closer she saw that it was some kind of black fabric. It was, in fact, a black hood made from a satiny material. The girl callously draped it over Janice's head. There was a drawstring on the opening, and the girl tightened it around Janice's throat. The world became black and Janice moaned in futile complaint. She felt the girl fiddling with her leash and then felt herself pulled over closer to the wall. The girl had shortened the lead on the leash and now Janice was forced up against the wall, with her breasts and her thighs pressed against it. She had to turn her head to avoid mashing her face.

"Mmmmmm!" Janice protested helplessly. The she heard the tell tale sound of the opening of the little whippy rod that all the women seemed to carry. Three burning lashes struck her rear globes. Janice whined at each one. "You must remain silent!" the girl instructed her in her most demanding voice.

The poor girl understood the instruction clearly. If she made any more noise, she would be whipped again. Despite her pain, despite her misery, Janice strained to comply. She wanted to cry, ball her eyes out, but she didn't want to be whipped. With a great strain, she suppressed her outward manifestations of her unhappiness and remained quiet.

It seemed a long time to Janice that she stood there, waiting for god knows what. She could see only blackness, but could hear the clickity click of the keyboard being struck, the phone when it buzzed and the secretary's polite, pleasing voice. Her nasty tones seemed reserved for Janice. The bound girl was self conscious of her nudity but was glad that at least her front was no longer visible to the girl. Once, while Janice was standing there helpless, she heard a buzzer go off and the door opening. There was an exchange of pleasantries between the secretary and another young woman in Japanese. The other young woman giggled and Janice concluded that they were talking about her. The secretary said something and the two young women laughed. The door opened and shut and the secretary went back to her computer.

Finally, the secretary got up and unhooked Janice's leash from the wall. Just before, there had been a buzz from the telephone and a brief conversation. The girl said, "*Hai!*" and put the telephone down.

When her leash was free from the wall, Janice was propelled by the young woman to a door in the room that Janice had seen when she first came in. She was dragged in a few steps and the leash was removed. The hood was untied at Janice's neck and removed as well. Her hands remained bound behind her.

Janice saw that she was standing in the middle of a finely decorated, modern office. It definitely had a woman's touch as there were several flowery prints and the walls were painted an extremely light shade of blue. There was a lamp on the long, wide desk with a small, frilly shade on it. Knick knacks covered the credenza behind the desk and the long deacon's table against the wall. The room smelled nice, too.

Behind the desk was sitting the Eurasian woman that Janice had met earlier in Kuribashi's office. There was a small pile of papers in front of her, sitting on the desk pad. Except for that, the blotter and the lamp, the desk was clear. The woman was looking at Janice intently. After a moment, she said to her, "Turn around."

Janice was ashamed to be naked in front of this attractive, well dressed, clearly sophisticated woman. She thought for a moment about resisting her control over her, but remembered the littlie whippy rod the women carried.

She complied with the order, turning around slowly until she again faced the woman. She had lovely eyes and a beauteous exterior which belied her obviously depraved nature. She had stood by, even assisted, in Janice's punishment and ravishment in Kuribashi's office. It was a stark reminder that goodness and beauty don't always go together.

"Number Four, you have been a lot of trouble so far. I want to start off with a clean slate with you now, but I warn you that there are extreme punishments that you will certainly suffer if your behavior continues. Do you understand?"

A cavern of fear opened in Janice's stomach. She wondered what an 'extreme punishment' would consist of. She had a vision of a medieval torture chamber with whips and chains and terrible devices. She nodded her head avidly.

"Good," the woman replied. "Now, I want you to stand up straight and spread your legs." Janice complied. "This is how you will stand when you come to my office or to anyone else's until you are told to perform a task or to present yourself otherwise. Understand?"

Janice nodded 'yes'.

"You will note that you have been given a new name, Number Four. You will respond to that name at all times. This is to emphasize to you your separation from your past life and your lowliness in status. Regardless of who you were, you are a new person now and must earn your right to have another name. For now, you are Number Four and nothing else." The woman paused to let this news sink in.

"My name is Ms. Yamamoto. I am in charge of comfort girl training for this facility. It is my function to ensure that you become a skilled and pliant sexual worker for the

Budikan Corporation. This will entail a rigorous regimen of training. Your progress will be assessed on a regular basis and if you are found wanting, you shall be punished. You must obey all of your superiors with alacrity and in a dutiful manner. At the beginning of each training period, you will receive five strokes of the cane."

This news particularly disconcerted the naked young girl. She started to whine a dismal protest, but remembered the reaction of the secretary and restrained it. Ms. Yamamoto had paused again for effect. She resumed.

"This is to serve as a graphic demonstration of our control over you, and to acclimate you to certain acts of physical entertainment that the users of your services may wish to indulge in. You will also accept certain physical alterations to your body that from time to time your superiors deem appropriate or to satisfy the wishes of an important user of your services.

"You have already met Mr. Tamarov. He has expressed an interest in you. He is in charge of comfort girl services in this market area and you may end up under his supervision when you are fully trained. You may expect that he will look in on you from time to time. The important thing to remember is that it is your duty to use your physical skills to please all of the users who are sent to you. Treat everyone with the same high level of attention to their needs and you will not disappoint anyone. Have I made myself clear?" the woman asked, finally.

Janice forlornly nodded her head 'yes'. What choice did she have? These people apparently had absolute power over her. Until she could find a way to escape, she would do everything that she needed to avoid unnecessary violence on her person.

Ms. Yamamoto shifted tack. "Now, you're going to have to complete this survey that you refused to fill out earlier. I'm going to undo your gag, but you will only speak in response to my questions, understood?"

Janice nodded her head again. She yearned to have the thick, leather gag removed from her mouth and she swore to herself not to violate the woman's instructions. The pretty, Eurasian woman got up from her chair and walked around the desk. She unfastened Janice's gag. "Put your legs wider apart," she ordered nonchalantly as she returned to her chair. Janice moved her feet to accommodate the mistress's instruction.

For the next twenty minutes, Janice revealed, in toto, all of her sexual experiences, fantasies and preferences. Ms. Yamamoto tut tutted when Janice described the kind of orgasms she preferred.

"I'm not surprised," the woman said. "Your test from this morning shows that you a woefully deficient in sexual response. You will have to work on that."

Janice was surprised at this news. She thought that she had responded, albeit unwillingly, with great vigor to her mechanical stimulation. The tittering of the young Japanese girls still echoed painfully in her head. How would she make herself more responsive, she wondered dolefully.

When the interview was over, Ms. Yamamoto got up and restored Janice's gag. She stood back and admired the bound young woman's flesh. "You're going to have to lose a few pounds, Number Four," the woman noted. "And we have some exercises that will firm up you breasts a little. I will have to discuss with Mr. Kuribashi whether to enlarge them or not. They are a little small."

She placed her hands on Janice's shoulders and turned her around. Janice quailed at the thought of surgery on her breasts. Wasn't any part of her to be left private? She had always thought them too big.

Ms. Yamamoto drew her hands over Janice's hips and over her rear globes. "Too many ice creams, Number Four. Well, that will stop right away," she commented. She measured her thighs with her hands and apparently was satisfied. "You have finely toned muscles, Number Four. That is good. Now lean over my desk and spread your legs."

Janice complied with some trepidation. She knew that the request must serve some purpose and that it was probably nothing that she would like. "Spread your legs," the woman ordered. "Wider," she emphasized when Janice meekly drew her legs apart.

The desk was just below the level of Janice's waist and when she placed her torso on it, it had the effect of raising her behind up in the air. Janice could feel cool air flowing over her nether lips as they were exposed to the other woman's view. Ms. Yamamoto stepped up behind the supine girl and placed her hand between her legs. Janice jumped slightly as she felt the woman's finger trace a line down between her sensitive lips. She had never been handled by a woman before and the lightness of the touch surprised her. The thought of participation in any lesbian acts was repulsive to her. Some of her girl friends had 'played around' with each other in high school, but she had always been appalled at the thought. And now she was bent over and exposed to this woman, apparently her mistress and she was making her pussy tingle.

Ms. Yamamoto drew her hand lightly over Janice's hairy mons. She caressed the inside of her thighs and over her ass. She then returned to the hairy bush and pressed the engorging lips together softly, massaging them, stroking the line of joinder of her thighs to her loins. Janice could feel her pulse quickening, her nipples stiffening as the woman expertly manipulated her. She felt it when the hand that was between her legs dipped its fingers into her crevasse and spread her moisture over her labial lips and over the hood that housed her bud of pleasure. It was getting hard with desire and a finger probed it, rubbing it gently.

Janice soon found herself reveling in the woman's touch. She had had so much fear and unhappiness as she listened to her mistress's lecture, and shame and embarrassment as she revealed her inner sexual self to her. She welcomed the chance to let her mind flow away, to dwell on the pleasurable sensations that the woman was bringing to her body. Her moan escaped her throat before she knew it. Her mind revolted momentarily as it recalled that her body was being used without her consent and in a manner that she thought to be depraved. But when the woman sank two of her fingers deep within her canal, rubbing the sensitive roof over it, she moaned again and let her aversions slide.

"Ohhhhhhh!' she moaned as the hand continued to enflame her. Her thighs began to quiver and her hips rotated as her passion was fed by the artful attentions to her slit. "Ohhhhhh!" she moaned again as the nubbin at its top was massaged by a gentle finger. She could feel her orgasm building. Her arms strained at the bonds that held them behind her back, useless to defend herself. Her breath became heavy and her body trembled. It was coming, it was coming, it was coming, and then it was there. Her pussy contracted in a hard throb as her orgasm overwhelmed her. She tried to fight it off, recalling that she was performing for this harsh, callous woman. But the waves of pleasure kept coming and she gave herself up to the crescendo of delight with a low, prolonged groan.

When the comfort girl's body ceased shuddering, Ms. Yamamoto stepped back and withdrew her hand. She wiped it on Janice's back side. "That was very unconvincing, Number Four. You have a lot of work to do." Janice heard the woman's comment through the haze of her post orgasmic bliss. She was humiliated at the show that she had put on for the elegant but terrible woman. She was chagrined that her orgasm, which had shook her innards, was not satisfactory.

"Please remain where you are," Ms. Yamamoto said pleasantly. "And put your legs together." Janice heard a closet door open and close and Ms. Yamamoto return to her spot behind her. The newly recruited comfort girl had drawn her legs together until they touched, happy to hide her still glowing cunt. As she brought her legs closer, her ass rose higher in the air.

"Now, don't move," the woman instructed Janice. "Or I'll give you five more."

"Five more?" thought Janice. "Five more what?"

Her answer came in a low 'whooshing' noise and a line of fire across her buttocks. "Ooooooooooooooo!" she cried, taken by surprise by the cruel blow.

Another blow followed the first quickly. "Ooooooooooooo!" Janice yelled into her gag again. This blow had struck the underside of her rear cheeks, just at the border between the back of her thighs and her ass. It burned like a brand and Janice's body shook with the pain. She wanted to get up and run from the cane wielding woman, but she recalled her ominous threat. She didn't want more than was absolutely necessary. With all her will, all her nerve, she remained as she was, her rear end presented to her mistress's pleasure.

"Whoosh! Crack!" A third stroke of the cane bit into Janice's thighs. Her feet danced in place as she tried to contain the hurt. Her wrists struggled at their confines, wanting more than anything to ward off the blows. "Oooooooooooh!" she cried again. "Eeeeeeese! Eeeeeeeeese! Op!" she yelled into her gag, her voice emerging as a sound slightly above a mumble. A fourth and then a fifth blow descended onto her buttocks. The girl was blubbering on the desk, her teardrops dampening the felt blotter. There was silence in the room aside from Janice's plaintive sobs. Was she done, she hoped. Was that five?

She was done. The Eurasian beauty picked up her telephone and uttered a crisp command into it. The door opened and the young secretary came in almost instantly. Words in Japanese were exchanged and she bowed to her boss. Ms. Yamamoto responded with a slight nod of her head, as befitted her superior stature in the company.

"Stand up, Number Four," Ms. Yamamoto ordered. It took a moment for the command to sink in but when Janice's beclouded mind deciphered it, she rose from the desk. Her face was awash with tears and her nose had run. Ms. Yamamoto barked an order to her underling. The secretary quickly got a tissue and wiped Janice's nose. Janice was glad for the favor. The secretary attached the leash again to Janice's collar, reinstalled her gag and took her from the room. As they left, Janice could hear the mistress of her fate talking on the telephone.

When they reached the anteroom, the secretary rehooked Janice to the wall, as tightly as before, and rehooded her. Janice heard the dreaded sound of the whippy rod being released. "What have I done now?" she wondered miserably. Four hard, rapid strokes sliced her rear end. It wasn't as bad as the cane, but it still stung like the blazes.

"You are a disgusting slut!" the secretary yelled at her. "You make a mess with your nose and I have to clean it up!" she remonstrated. "Do not do this again!"

Janice pressed her body against the wall. She contemplated her future life, full of misery and abuse. She wanted desperately to cry, but feared more punishment from the pretty, black haired secretary. Hatred welled up in her, for Ms. Yamamoto, Mr. Kuribashi, Mr. Tomarov and especially for this heartless girl. How she wished that she could get her hands on one of the whippy rods. She would whip the girl's back raw.

But that was just as likely as Janice being able to effectuate an escape. In other words, no chance at all.

勢覇

CHAPTER SIX
LESSONS

Her first stop after her introductory lecture from Ms. Yamamoto was the large, communal bathroom. It was tiled in a dark, almost black, green and had a spacious sunken tub. The faucets and spouts were of bright, golden brass. There was no one else in it when they arrived and Janice stood by while the middle aged woman filled the tub with hot water. She poured a generous portion of sweet smelling bath oil in it, loosened Janice's wrists from behind her back and unbuckled her gag from behind her head. She removed her kimono, revealing her own, taut and shapely flesh and a black, hairy bush. She led the girl down several steps and into the pool-like tub. While the tub was large, it was also shallow. Standing in it, the water reached to just above Janice's knees.

The water was very hot, and Janice did a little dance while her lower legs and feet acclimated themselves to it. The matron demonstrated with her own body how Janice should lie on her back against a wall of the tub and let the steamy, oily water spread over her body. Janice lowered her self slowly, letting the heat of her skin match the water before settling down. It was soothing to the embattled girl. She let the heat of the water and the sweet smell of the bath oil seep into her. It was almost heaven after the terrible stress, tension and pain she had suffered in a very short time. She wondered what time it was outside of her prison. Was it the same day as when she was picked up from her apartment house by the limousine? Was it night? Early morning? Her estimate was obfuscated by the time she had spent locked in her cage in the darkness. There were no windows and no contact with the outside. The training facility was its own little world.

Janice luxuriated in the soothing warmth of the tub for quite a while. Her matron lay across from her and several times turned the hot water back on so as to keep the temperature of the pool up. After a while, she floated over to where Janice lay and motioned for her to dip her long, brown hair into the water. Janice slid her body towards the center of the tub and let her head sink below the surface. The sensation of being underwater drove away even further the horrible events of her day. Her hair floated around her head in a silky morass. She let herself drift there, her eyes closed, all of the oppressive details of her travails miles away. She was suspended in a nether land of peace and sensual delight. But, eventually, her reverie had to end as the need for a fresh lungful of air became emergent. When she surfaced, face first, her long, brown hair lay sleek and flat against her head and back. The matron had retrieved a bottle of shampoo and, after instructing Janice to kneel up, massaged the frothing substance into her scalp. Her hands were strong, but gentle. She soaped up the long skein of hair that descended down Janice's back. When she was done, she washed the soap away thoroughly with a hose. Janice closed her eyes and let the water flow over her head and down her body. She was relaxed now, at relative peace. She would endure her torments somehow. She knew that now. Somehow, she would get through it.

The matron worked a conditioner into the hair. It had a hint of jasmine to it and Janice breathed the smell in appreciatively. Then the two women stood and the matron began to wash her body.

The hands of the matron searched every inch of Janice's flesh. Using a bar of plain white soap containing a skin softener, she rubbed a soft washcloth over Janice's pretty breasts, her belly and her behind. She made Janice lean over with her hands on the top of the tub and washed her hairy slit. It was odd, thought Janice, that so much tenderness and, what seemed almost like affection, should be mixed with the cruelty and hardness of her imprisonment. The matron, who earlier had felt no compunction about whipping her with her steel rod, pressed her own naked flesh up against Janice's body sensually while she soaped her neck and her face. When she was done, she rinsed Janice off, being careful to clean the soap from her loins. She then ordered the sparkling clean girl to sit back on the edge of the tub, her legs dangling over the side.

The naked matron stepped from the tub and returned with a small brush, a bowl of hot water and a double bladed safety razor. She placed the materials on the side of the tub and instructed Janice to lay on her back. Janice palled at what she thought was about to happen. She had heard of women who shaved their pubic hairs, but had never wanted to shave her own. It was like a badge of maturity and it seemed silly to return her sex to a prepubescent state. She had seen one or two women in the locker-room at the exercise club that she went to who had removed all of their lower hair. She had wondered, briefly, what it would feel like to rub her hand along the denuded loins, but had put the thought out of her mind quickly as inappropriate.

The production of the shaving materials was a stark reminder to Janice that she was not a pampered guest here, but a slavish whore. She was a prisoner upon whom anything could be visited. They called her an 'employee' but she was really property. Someone, perhaps Ms. Yamamoto, or maybe Mr. Kuribashi, or even someone higher up, if there was any such person, had decided that their sex slaves should have bare cunts. And so, she would too.

The matron's whippy stick was in her kimono, several arm lengths away. For a second, Janice thought of running over and grabbing it and forcing the woman to let her out of the locked bathroom, to make her call the elevator and help her escape. But then she thought of the 'extreme' punishment promised by Ms. Yamamoto and released the thought. Besides, the matron seemed strong and probably had considerable experience in dealing with recalcitrant young women. Doubtless she would disarm Janice in a second and then where would she be? No, this was not a good opportunity to escape. There would be a better one sometime, she hoped.

Once her loins were lathered with a soapy shaving cream, the older woman began to stroke the curly, brown hairs away. Janice felt vulnerable and exposed as she lay back on the cool tiles with her knees up and her legs spread. Her ass hung out slightly over the edge of the tub and the woman had no problem in accessing every square inch of Janice's sex. Her hands were firm, yet gentle as they pushed and pulled at her intimate flesh to access the unwanted growth. Several times, she looked up at the supine girl, smiling, as if engaged in some secret conspiracy with her. It was a strange sensation to feel the sharp razor pull over her skin. As the hair was scraped away, her pussy became cooler, the effect of the air on her now bare sex.

The room was filled with the steam from the bath and Janice lost herself momentarily in the fog. What strange things were happening to her. To think that she was deep within an ordinary office building, probably only miles from her apartment. All around her, within ten feet of her up or down, there were probably regular people doing regular work day things. It was like she had entered another dimension, one parallel with her old one, the one populated by secretaries, clerks, executives and the like, and had been captured by some strange tribe. The fog made this seem all the more probable as it distorted everything around her.

When the comfort girl's loins were fully denuded, the matron rubbed a soothing lotion over the irritated skin. She rubbed it over Janice's plump labia, around the sides of them and over her lower belly. It seemed to Janice that the hands were lingering just a little too long than was necessary to accomplish their task. The hands glided up the insides of her thighs and back down over her hairless slit. Gentle, light fingers began to stroke her lower lips while the other hand stroked her lower belly. She heard the water in the tub splash as the matron changed position and moved closer between her outstretched thighs. Janice revolted at what seemed to be coming and tried to sit up and move away. Her escape from the woman's caresses was halted by a short, sharp command from the woman. With bitter resignation, Janice lay back and let events take their course.

When she felt the woman's hot tongue slide up the length of her moistening gash, Janice felt a sinking feeling in her gut. A woman was supping at her soft, sensitive sex and, in spite of her aversion to female to female sex, her pussy had already begun to burn with need. The fervent tongue pushed deeply into her tender canal while the mouth fixed itself over her love lips. The woman's hands tantalized her body, rubbing the delicate inside of her thighs, coursing over her belly, tweaking the nipples of her breasts. The combination of the relaxing residue of her bath and the delicious sensations being delivered to her brain by the active tongue and lips of the older woman melted Janice into a puddle. She had no strength and, frankly, no will, to resist the developing urgency of her passion. The heat of the woman's breath on her leaking hole while her tongue traced the space between her engorged and distended lower lips sent Janice into ecstasy. When she captured her stiff clit with her lips and sucked at it softly, Janice moaned with pleasure.

The tile walls of the bathroom echoed back to Janice her involuntary expressions of lust. She reached out a hand and, letting it come to rest on the busy head of the matron, made a weak attempt to push the head away. It was if she could excuse her growing appreciation of the woman's efforts if she made at least a desultory attempt to suppress it.

The woman teased Janice's sex, prolonging her passion. She seemed intuitively able to discern when Janice was ready to crest the mountain of her lust. The woman would pull back her tongue, run it around the sides of the hairless cunt and then return to her task, recommencing Janice's drive to orgasm. Finally, she let the young woman come. She planted her lips firmly on Janice's pleasure bud and taunted it with little flicks of her tongue. Janice groaned and her body began to shake and convulse. The woman wrapped her arms tightly around her thighs, pinning her lower torso in place. Janice cried out at each wrenching contraction of her womb, calling out, "Oh! Oh! Oh! Oh!" as the throbs of her pussy sent waves of pleasure through her body. "Oh! Oh! Oh! Oh!" she called out, her voice echoing throughout the dark green tiled room while the agile tongue drove her lust.

Once her convulsions had subsided, the older woman let Janice lay there, her spent legs now lying listlessly over the edge of the pool, as she put away the shaving materials and dried off her own body. She replaced her kimono and then pulled out her whippy stick and clicked the telescoped rod open. Janice heard the tell tale sound and snapped out of her dreamy state. The woman tapped her on the thigh with the end of the steel whip and Janice struggled to her feet. Her gag was restored, her wrists reconfined behind her back, the short leash reconnected to her collar. In moment, she was back to being an abject prisoner. The matron keyed in the combination on the lock, swiped her plastic card and led Janice from the room. When she had returned Number Four to her cell, she ordered her back into her cage, locked it and left. A second after the door closed, the lights went out.

* * * * * * * * * * * * *

There was no routine to her training. It seemed to concentrate on three things, her depersonalization, through confinement and harsh usage, discipline, through the application of the many varieties of whips and canes to her flesh, and the development of her sensual experience, by the frequent and regular stimulation of her body to orgasm.

Sometimes she would spend what seemed like hours trapped in her cage, sometimes it seemed like minutes. During some intervals, the dim, overhead light would be off, during others, it was on. Sometimes it would go on and then off again for no apparent reason without any change in her status. She would kneel in the center of the room, her hands on her head, her firm and desirable breasts presented to the ever-present eye of the camera. Then the light would go on that transmitted an order to return to her cage and then, after a while, without rhyme or reason, the other one ordered her out again.

She had been instructed, on her personal trainer's first visit, in the meaning of the lights on the wall under the camera lens. When the red one came on, she was to go and lock herself in the cage. The cage was connected to an electrical signal which locked and unlocked it remotely, and when the blue one came on, she was to emerge from her tiny steel prison and kneel in the center of the room, as she was now, her legs spread and her hands locked behind her head. A yellow light meant that she should roll out the thick, queen sized, cotton futon and kneel on it, her hands resting palms up on her thighs. A trainer, was coming to have sex with her.

When the green light was on, and it was rare, she could relax, take a drink of water, pee. She was charged with taking meticulous care of her cell and she wiped and dusted every chance that she got. She had been punished severely twice for smudges of sweat found on the floor.

And she received her five strokes regularly. Her primary trainer was an Asian man of small stature. He introduced himself as Mr. Tanaka. Janice was to call him *Tanakasama* as a sign of respect. In spite of being short, he was actually a few inches shorter than Janice, he was well muscled and strong. When he gripped her arm or leg, or pushed her onto her back to fuck her and forced her knees up almost touching her shoulders, she felt his compact strength in his arms, his thighs and his hips.

The matron took care of all her physical needs. Aside from washing her and feeding her, it had been apparently laid to her to assist Janice in the development of her sexual responses. Her hands always seemed to be on the girl. She kissed her breasts and her lips, insinuating her tongue into her mouth. Janice existed in a state of almost perpetual sexual arousal when she was present. She never left the room, unless a client or trainer had come in to use her, without stroking the comfort girl trainee to orgasm.

Janice was perturbed the first time the woman forced her to lay down on the soft, matted floor and began to caress her body. Janice's hands were joined together and were tied off over her head and attached to a ring in the wall. Her gag was left in. The nameless matron used her lips and hands to drive the young woman to distraction. She suckled at her breasts, fondled the cleft between her thighs, kissed and licked her belly. When Janice seemed ready to come, she relented her sensual torment and let the girl squirm and moan, her need for completion frustrated. She would repeat this exercise many times, until Janice was frantic with need, her body begging for sexual release.

It was during their third session that the matron shocked Janice by producing a long, thick penis shaped object. It was jet black and was attached to a leather harness. Janice stared at its bulbous head as the matron, who had discarded her kimono, fastened the device around her hips.

The newly minted comfort girl was kneeling in the middle of the small room with her hands on her head. After locking her wrists to the ring in her collar, the black and gray haired matron pushed her over to her back and crept between her thighs. Janice knew what she was going to do and she pleaded miserably behind her gag for the woman to absolve her from this lurid and depraved usage. But the matron paid her no mind. She raised Janice's knees with her hands and began to stroke the inside of her thighs. She kissed them, letting her tongue drag flat across the tender flesh. Her hand began to tease the flesh between them. When she was satisfied that the girl was properly lubricated, she edged forwards until the tip of the large device was pressing against the girl's moist entrance.

The plastic prick was cool as it began to part Janice's lower lips. Its surface was covered with little ridges and Janice felt them scour lightly the walls of her sheath. It soon warmed to her flesh and the matron began to saw in and out of Janice's hot tunnel. Janice lay atop the hands that were locked behind her neck. At first the experience of being fucked with an artificial instrument was grossly disconcerting, but soon the unhappy girl's attention was devoted solely to the mesmerizing waves of pleasure floating up from her filled pussy.

The matron gave the girl long, slow, leisurely strokes. Her chest rested on Janice's and her small breasts lay mashed against the fuller, more voluptuous ones of the comfort girl. Her tongue teased Janice's throat, and the sensation of her wet muscle floating over her sensitive flesh made Janice shiver with pleasure.

But it was the false cock which was master. Janice found herself thrusting back at it as her passion grew higher and higher. Her heels dug firmly into the soft, rubberized pad that served as her cell's floor, her jaw gripped the thick, leather plug in her mouth tightly. She felt the other woman's hands undo the buckle to her gag and remove it. She immediately pressed her lips against the young woman's and swirled her tongue deep within her mouth.

The men who had fucked her since she had been a prisoner took her with little or no concern for her personal pleasure. Often, despite her deep yearning not to, she would orgasm as a result of their efforts. But their thrusts were hard, forceful, dominating. They used their cocks like a weapon and grinned at her as they forced her to moan as they rode her. If she was made to come, it was for their amusement or gratification. But copulation with her matron was a totally different thing. The whole intent and purpose was the girl's sexual stimulation. And the plowing of her hairless furrow was done with deliberate, long, generous strokes. The rhythm of the woman's hips, slow and leisurely, was both a pleasure and a torment to the girl. Each time the serrated surface of the plastic cock ran the length of her womb, rubbed across its dilated entrance, Janice sighed with unwanted pleasure.

When Janice's orgasm began, telegraphed by the sudden tenseness of her body, her arching back, her deep, lustful moan into the mouth of her tormenter, the matron began to piston her hips hard and fast into the steaming cunt. She freed Janice's mouth and she began to nip and lick at her stiff nipples.

"Oh, god! Oh, god," the girl called out, her mouth free to express her reactions to the intense, mind wrenching contractions of her pussy. "Oh, yes! Oh, yes!" she cried. Her legs circled the back of the older woman's lower legs and she pulled them in towards her. She bucked and heaved as the pleasurable sensations ran through her.

When her lusts began to fade, she expected the matron to cease the abuse of her now lush and pouting sex. But, other than a pause to resume her rhythm, the matron kept going.

Janice began to beg the woman to stop. Her only multiorgasmic experience had been while under attack by that dreadful machine when she had first arrived at her training center. She had always exerted too much control for that to happen, waiting patiently for her lover to climax before letting herself go. This had made for some very frustrating couplings, as many times the male had exhausted his forces and slumped in her arms before she had had a chance to come. But it was the price she paid, she thought, for maintaining control of her own body, of keeping her lustful feelings within limits that she could assert.

But now, she had no control. The heat of the matron's body accelerated the rekindling of her need. "Please, no, please no," Janice mumbled even as her pussy welcomed the relentless ever hard prick. "Ohhhhhh!" she moaned as she used her shapely, well toned legs to try and push herself away from her tormentor. But the woman held on tight to her and soon Janice was overwhelmed by another series of deep shudders as she climaxed once again.

Janice, out of breath, her cunt still pulsing with diminishing pleasure, her whole body aglow, felt the woman withdraw the steely, black instrument from her. She sighed as she felt it leave. But then the woman grabbed at her right arm and her hip and skillfully pushed her first to her side and then to her stomach. "Kneel!" the woman commanded curtly, slapping her rear end. Janice had learned to obey the matron's commands without thought of refusal. She had suffered the woman's short temper too many times. She drew her knees up under her. The matron's strong hands kept her torso leaning over, Janice's forehead pressed against the soft, slick mat, and then spread her legs. When she felt the tip of the matron's tool pressing at her flush gate from behind, Janice moaned with unhappiness. This was not the way it was supposed to be. She had been taught to curb her lusts, to deplore wantonness. As the black prick separated her nether lips once again and plunged into her depths, she began to cry.

The relentless strokes of the hard, merciless cock, soon had Janice panting and squirming with passion. Somehow, her mind disappeared and her body did all the thinking for her. It trembled and shook as she came and thrust her hips back at the invader. She heard herself yell and scream as she climaxed again. The matron, too, cried out, as the pressure of the end of the dildo, rubbing against her own nub of pleasure, drove her over the cliff. She grabbed the comfort girl's shoulders and thrust at her again and again, gaining maximum friction on her stiff clit as she came.

At the third mind numbing orgasm, the matron was satisfied. She pulled the black beastie from Janice's cunt slowly, her body still enjoying the afterglow of her climax. "Up, up," she ordered her charge. Obediently, but with much effort, Janice brought her limp, pleasured body to an upright kneeling position.

"Turn around," the matron barked out. When Janice had turned to face her, the matron proffered the slick, wet, plastic, faux penis to her mouth. "Clean!" the matron commanded. Janice had to think what the matron meant. How could she clean anything with her hands bound? But then the matron shoved the big, black cock at her lips. "Clean!" she ordered in a more emphatic voice. Janice could see the remnants of her leakage on the device. Her stomach turned at that thought of consuming it. But the matron had ordered it and she was not willing to put her squeamishness over the matron's wrath. She hesitatingly opened her mouth and circled the plastic manhood obediently with her lips. The matron pushed it in until it pressed against her throat, held it there until Janice began to gag and choke and then withdrew it slowly, Janice's lips pursed obediently tightly around it. The matron stood and dressed. She picked up the discarded gag from the floor and reinstalled it in Janice's mouth, buckling the strap tightly behind her head. She pulled her whippy rod out of her kimono and opened it with a 'click'. Tapping it against Janice's thigh, she stated flatly, "In cage." Dutifully, the aftermath of her wild orgasmic episode still resonating in her body, the young woman obeyed.

* * * * * * * * * * *

Several times, Tanakasama was accompanied by one or two of the other trainers. The first time, Janice was kneeling in the center of the room, her hands behind her head in response to the command of the blue light. She had been there for some time and her arms ached from the demanding position. As she saw her trainer enter, she heard humored, male voices behind him. Two more men entered the small cell. The men were all Asian, dressed in the signature green and red silk kimonos of the trainers. A matron followed them into the room carrying a small, rectangular, short footed table, lacquered in black and gold. On top of it was a tray containing a large flask of steaming sake and several small cups. She placed it down gracefully and then left.

The men seemed to ignore Janice at first, throwing off their kimonos, and sitting naked and cross legged around the table, shooting back cupfuls of the hot liquor, talking and laughing with each other. Janice just knelt and waited nervously for their pleasure. She had received her five strokes of the cane several hours ago and the red traces of her wounds were still evident across her breasts. Her stomach churned at the prospect of her ravishment by all three of the callous, hard looking men. Her arms ached from their prolonged positioning and her body swayed from fatigue. Her nipples were hard with fear and her throat felt constricted. She cast a sidelong glance at the men, apparently oblivious to her existence. These men were going to use her, of that she was sure. Would they whip her? Would they hurt her?

Finally, her trainer called her over. The frightened girl crawled to his side. He removed her thick, leather gag and issued the harsh, guttural command for her to suck his prick. Leaning over his right thigh, she took his soft cock in her hand and brought it to her mouth. Her head was buried in the man's lap. He leaned back to give her better access to his cock. Slowly, the round head of his manhood began to swell in her mouth and the stem of the rod begin to stiffen and expand. Janice absorbed his salty taste as she swirled her tongue around the underside of the fat helmet. The man to her trainer's right placed his hand between her legs and began to stroke her bare, fleshy lips. Dutifully, Janice spread her legs to accommodate him.

The comfort girl's breasts rubbed against her trainer's thigh as her head bobbed at its task. The hand on her sex began to enflame her and she gave a little moan, the vibration of which was transferred to her trainer's stiff pole. The men all laughed when they heard it and exchanged witty comments.

As Janice continued at her task, the other men continued to drink the sake and maintained a lively conversation in Japanese. Her trainer placed his hand on the back of her neck and pressed her head down until the bulbous end of his cock passed into her throat. Janice coughed and gagged, but the strong hand kept her firmly in place. She had started to whine and shake for want of oxygen when the hand relented and let her raise her head. She sucked air deeply into her lungs and opened her mouth obediently when the hand forced her down again.

Janice was grateful when she felt her trainer stiffen and his cock begin to throb. The thick prick filled her mouth and throat as the man grunted his satisfaction at her efforts. The bitter tasting spunk filled her oral cavity and lined her throat as the man pumped her head up and down on his loins. With one great shout of pleasure, he shot the remnants of his discharge into her.

Janice fully expected to service the other men similarly, and was surprised when the man to her trainer's right got to his feet and stepped over to the small cabinet sunk into the wall. Janice knew that the cabinet contained instruments for the purposes of inflicting pain and she whimpered lowly. The man returned with a 4' length of thin, nylon rope. He ordered Janice to the center of the room and fastened her hands behind her back by clipping her bracelets together. Her trainer tossed him her gag and he reinserted it into her mouth. He ran the rope through a ring in the front of her collar and pushed her head down to the floor. Walking behind her, he knelt down and forced her thighs apart with his strong hands. He reached under her and captured the two ends of the rope.

The girl trembled as she wondered what the man had in mind for her. She felt one end of the rope being tied around a ring in the leather bracelet around her right ankle. The man pulled on the other end of the rope and Janice felt her head being forced down between her knees. The man pulled the rope until her head was pulled back towards her ankles as far as it would go. Janice's back curved to accommodate the strain on her neck. The top of her head rested on the floor and she could see her widespread thighs and her vulnerable sex. She watched as the man tied the other end of the rope to her left ankle.

The strain on her back and neck became painful almost immediately. She shuddered when the man gave her a mighty celebratory slap on her rear cheeks. The other men cooed their admiration of the man's resourcefulness.

The man who had tied her returned to the little table and, after making a toast, shot back a cupful of sake. He returned to the bound girl and ran his hands over her strained back, her buttocks and between her thighs. His hand found her crevasse and he manipulated it until it was distended and wet. Insinuating himself between her legs, he rubbed his hardened prick along the gap between her nether lips. Satisfied that the slit was properly lubricated, he slid his stiff prick inside her.

Janice sighed as the cock penetrated her. In spite of her dismal contortion, she felt herself responding as the man ploughed her wet hole. Her head upside down, she could actually see his cock slithering in and out of her canal, his heavy testicles swinging back and forth as he thrust slowly in and out of her. His strong, rough hands had hold of her hips and he used this to hold her body still while he pressed his own hips into her. He was taking his time, enjoying the grasp of Janice's tight tunnel on his cock, listening to her squeals of pain as her back and neck muscles were driven to their extremes. He was waiting for the comfort girl to respond to his labors. Her pussy continued to moisten and distend and Janice's exclamations of pain became ones of pleasure.

She hated herself for succumbing to the man's efforts. Something about his total control of her body excited her. She was being used as a receptacle for his cock. Nothing was demanded of her other than her hot moisture and the soft, tender flesh of her canal. If self control of her sexual urges had been her lodestar prior to her recruitment, she was at the apotheosis of the opposite now. She could not move a single muscle voluntarily. She could not prevent the callous use of her body, revolt against her abuse, even if she had the courage to do so. Her pussy was afire and she could feel her body prepare for sharp, intense spasms of delight. She moaned into her gag, her bound hands clenched tightly into little fists.

As her cunt began to throb and pulse with pleasure, she could hear the voices of the other men expressing their admiration for the results produced by the man at her rear. The man's passion reached its own peak and he began to slam his belly hard against her rear cheeks as he drove his orgasm on. His moans mixed with hers as they both came, his body slamming hard into hers, hers, trembling and shaking in her confines.

When the man who had just fucked her withdrew, the third man crawled up behind her. He took his turn at exploring the surface of her firm buttocks and thighs. He reached between her legs and pinched and squeezed her defenseless breasts. Then, thrusting two fingers deep into her yawning pussy, he gathered her moisture onto his fingers.

When Janice felt the fingers begin to probe her small, tight anal ring, her heart began to thump in her chest. This was a moment that she had been expecting, but feared. Her trainer had not used her there, although he had explored it with his fingers while he ran his cock in and out of her vagina. She knew that he or someone else would want to use the narrow passage. She had never tried anal sex and the thought of it appalled her. A wave of misery flowed through her as she realized that the moment of truth had come at last.

The man behind the bound and unhappy young woman turned to speak to Janice's trainer in Japanese as he explored the brown star between Janice's rear cheeks.

"*Matsui, are you telling me that you haven't fucked her here yet?*" he asked.

"*I've been saving it for you, Benji,*" he replied. "It'll be nice and tight and the whore will squeal like a stuck pig. I knew that you would enjoy being her first."

Benji laughed. "*I am in your debt, Tanaka-san,*" he said.

Benji turned to the matter at hand. He had used his fingers to stretch the soft, pliant tissue around the small hole. Janice uttered a long, miserable moan from behind her gag as she felt the fingers inside her. She struggled at her bindings feverishly as she sought to evade the depraved man's violation. The fingers withdrew and she felt the man's thighs rub against the back of hers. Whereas the prior man had lowered his hips and thrust up into her sex, this man knelt up on his knees and prepared to enter her bowels more forthrightly. She felt the thick, hot head of his cock press against the dainty ring. She felt the slow, but strong pressure on it as the man began to force his way in. She felt the tissue stretch to accommodate him and then an intense burning as the delicate flesh around the hard, thick tool tore and cracked.

"Ooooooooooooooh!" she moaned as the pain coursed through her. "Ooooooooooooooh! Op! Op! Eeeeeeese! Oooo-ooooh!" Her neck and back strained as her body shook in protest of the man's penetration of her bowels. "Ooooooooooh!"

Matsui and the other man laughed and toasted their friend and coworker at the vocal results of his assault. Her sounds were muffled, but her meaning was clear. What did she expect, that this pleasing resource of her body would be left untapped? She would learn to ass fuck and like it. Matsui made a mental pledge to himself to get her accommodated to this usage as soon as possible.

Janice continued to moan and groan as the man rasped his hard and thick cock across the injured tissue. She could see his naked, hairless, well muscled thighs between hers. His cock filled her in a way she had never experienced. It was a detestable presence in her, while at the same time producing a whole new sensuous experience. Her rear muscles strained to expel him, but only served to grasp his manhood tighter.

Benji closed his eyes and let himself enjoy the sound of the woman's distress and the tightness of the ring around the shaft of his rod. His cock was sunk into her murky warmth. He felt his fluids building and increased the pace of his thrusts accordingly. He groaned as he came, pumping his spunk deep inside the helpless, forlorn woman. When his forces were expended, he withdrew.

The girl continued a piteous, low moan even after her assault had ended. Benji grabbed a cup of sake and proposed a toast.

"Here's to the opening of a new route to pleasure," he cried. Janice's rear entrance still gaped from its use and Benji poured half of his cup of the still warm sake into it. The alcohol burned the torn tissue and Janice cried and moaned. Benji and the other men laughed and downed another round.

Janice did not know how long the men stayed. It seemed like they were there for hours. The drinking continued. She remained as she was, bound grotesquely, for a long time until one of the men released her. They used her intermittently, fucking her mouth and her cunt as the whim took them, one or two at a time. They beat her for their enjoyment. Benji used her rear hole again, this time while she was on her back, her knees pressed up into her chest, her wrists bound together behind her, helpless to protect her. He smiled at her as tears poured down her face and cries of pain and unhappiness emerged from her gagged mouth.

* * * * * * * * * * *

Things were not quite the same for Janice after her session with the three trainers. When they left her, stuffed in her little cage, she cried and cried until, mercifully, she fell asleep. Heretofore, Janice had felt that her status here was somehow temporary. That she would escape, or be freed, or something. In any case, she refused to believe that she was a permanent bond servant of the Budikan Corporation. But, when she awoke to hear the little chimes set to announce the turning on of the blue light, which meant that someone was coming for her and she should leave her cage, she knew that henceforth in her life she would be subject to the whims of others, that she would have no rights, and that she would suffer an endless travail of abuse.

It was the matron who came. She sensed that Janice had had a rough time of it during her session with the trainers, and she was especially gentle and kind to the young woman. She took her to the bathing room and let her soak for a long time. She handled her body delicately and prolonged her oral caresses after her shave until the unhappy girl screamed out her desire.

When they returned to her cell, Janice was feeling a little better. Her body was relaxed and at ease and her mind had been cleared. If her life had been changed unalterably, there was only one thing to do, find a way to accept what she had become. She had never experienced sex like she had experienced it since her kidnapping, if you could call it that. Her surrender, that's what it really was. She had turned herself in, submitted to these people's will, succumbing to their greater force.

Since her surrender, she had been ploughed, fingered, stroked with ardent lips and tongues. Ms. Yamamoto had criticized her for her lack of sexual response, but what would she say about her now? She was ready to give herself wholly over to the pleasures that she could find. She had become a sexual being, a type of super woman.

Janice's resolve to embrace the sensuality of her new life was soon put to the test. The next training period, after her ritualistic bath, when she entered her cell, the gray haired man, the one Ms. Yamamoto had called Tamarov, was sitting on her futon, cross legged, awaiting her. He had already shucked his clothes and was drinking tea from a tiny cup. The matron made a suitable bow and fled. Janice was left standing in front of the slave master, her hands bound behind her and her mouth gagged. Tamarov placed the delicate cup down on a small, lacquered table next to him and stood up. He bowed slightly to the frightened woman. She dutifully returned the bow, making sure that she bowed lower than him. He stepped forward and unlocked Janice's gag. He turned her around and released her hands.

"Kneel on the futon," he ordered her.

Janice fell to her knees and crawled over to where the well built gray haired man indicated. She knelt up, her back straight, her knees wide apart and her hands palm upwards on her thighs. She bowed her head in deference to the man's greater power.

"*Konishiwa, Nanba-shi,*" he said to her. "Greetings, Number Four."

"*Konishiwa, Shukunsama,*" Janice replied. "Greetings, Master."

"I've come to see how you have been progressing, Number Four. Have you been learning your lessons well?" he asked her

"Yes, Master," she replied, nervously. After all, this was the first man to beat her when she arrived. He might decide to do it again.

"Come closer to me," he ordered.

Janice walked on her knees over to the man until her knees just touched his. He reached out and placed his hands on her breasts. Her nipples were already stiff, either with fear or incipient passion, Janice didn't know. The man's hands were rough and hot. She leaned over to present her delicate, firm and ample globes to him. He grasped them firmly with his large hands and took his pleasure with them, rolling them through his hands, pinching the sensitive nipples, squeezing them tightly. He watched the girl's face while he handled her; Janice knew what he would find there, for the prospect of her ravishment by this hard, cruel man had sparked her desire.

As she had promised herself, she didn't fight it. All scruples and morality regarding sex had been cast aside. The laws of society clearly did not apply here. She was free to relish her passion, let her lust run free. She licked her lips and stared back at the man. Her eyes had softened and her breathing had become deep. It was no act. The hands that held her breasts were sending delicious waves of pleasure through her. She closed her eyes and sighed.

"Give me your lips," Tamarov said. Janice pushed her head forwards so that her lips could meet his. His tongue entered her mouth and she welcomed it fervently. She could feel her pussy tingle as their tongues danced together. She pressed her lips up against his hard and moaned. She placed her hands, which had remained on her thighs, on his and probed his strong muscles with her fingers.

Tamarov pulled Janice down on her side and he followed her to the soft, cotton surface of the futon. Their bodies stretched out together and he rolled onto his back.

"Pleasure me," he said.

The dim light of her cell softened the hard man's features. She slid her hands across his strong, taut chest and applied her lips to his skin. The taste of his flesh enflamed her. She spread her body over his, dragging her heavy, blood filled breasts across his chest. She pushed her right leg between his and pressed her moistened slit hard against his thigh. She moaned as she felt his heat against her pussy. She wanted this man. He had raped her and beat her, and his invitation to fuck had not been a mere suggestion. But she wanted him nonetheless. She wanted to hear him moan and sigh under her caresses, wanted to feel his body squirm with passion.

The impassioned comfort girl slid her hand down Tamarov's flat belly and descended to his loins. Her mouth had seized on one of his nipples and she teased the little point with her teeth as her hand encircled his cock. The strength and girth of his manhood sent a thrill through the lustful girl. How long ago had it been, she thought, since the thought of a hot, hard cock in her hand had been just a barely tolerable prelude to a frustrating act of coitus. How long had she been a prisoner? She had no way of telling. Her hair was trimmed regularly, or at least what appeared regularly. Her loins were made bare every time she bathed. Even her fingernails were clipped. The only way that her body could measure the passage of time was through her monthly scourge. But, she supposed, they could have taken care of that too. Certainly they had put some kind of birth control in her food, of that she was sure. She couldn't conceive of them wanting her pregnant.

She softly stroked the captured, fleshy instrument. She felt the man's body melt beneath her. It was ironic. She was the slave, but, yet, she was the one in control. She was managing this master's lust. True, he had surrendered it to her, but for the next ten or fifteen minutes, or however long she could manage to keep him on the brink of climax, he was hers.

As the lustful young woman slipped her lips across the tight skin of Tamarov's abdomen, she cupped his heavy, wrinkled sac in her hand. Her lips met the hairy base of his instrument and ascended the stiff pole until they had captured its fat head. The man groaned as she moved her head down, gradually and deliberately, until the thick, hot rod was plunged deep into her mouth.

He was so vulnerable, she thought. She could wreak her revenge on him for his cruel and callous treatment of her right now. She could smash the soft stones that she was slowly manipulating, tear and rip at his manhood with her teeth. He would retaliate, of that she was sure, but she would have struck back at her tormentors. The thought passed quickly though, and she began to lose herself in the sensual experience of servicing the desires of the man's hard, strong body.

Tamarov moaned as Janice buried his cock in the edge of her throat. He groaned as she drew her lips up and down his shaft, clamped tightly around it, again and again. She ran her tongue teasingly over the small opening at its tip until his hips began to writhe beneath her.

Her own sex was burning with need. She lifted her leg over his body and squatted above him, her lush envelope poised to receive his member. Guiding it with her right hand, she lowered herself, impaling herself on the sturdy pole. A wave of lust ran through her as she eased the stiff prick into her. Tamarov's hands grabbed her hips tightly. He face was a mask of pleasurable torment as Janice's pussy absorbed his meat. When she possessed his rod to its hilt, as she had been taught, she tightened the soft muscles of her canal and lifted her hips, stroking Tamorov's cock with her cunt.

Slowly, the lust driven young woman raised and lowered herself on the hot member. Her head was thrown back and her eyes jammed tight as thrill after thrill coursed through her. She wanted desperately to come, to allow the sharp pangs of pleasure to drive her wild. But she knew that she had to wait until Tamarov signaled his readiness. Her hands rested on his strong, muscular chest as she continued to rock her hips. "Ahhhhhhhhhhh!" she moaned as her pussy vibrated with sensation.

And then Tamarov's grip on her hips tightened. He began to thrust back at her. He groaned and his body tensed. He was coming. When the first throb of his thick, long cock reverberated through her sensitized sex, Janice let herself go. She cried out as her contractions sent wave after wave of electrified pleasure through her. She felt the man's hot spunk emptying inside her and she moaned, her thighs gripping his hips firmly, her cunt grabbing the spurting cock tightly. "Arrrrrrrgh! Arrrrrrgh! Arrrrrrgh!" the man exclaimed, his hips thrusting his prick deeply inside of the impassioned girl. "Arrrrrgh! Arrrrrrrgh! he cried. His hands released the hips of the squirming convulsing female and took hold of her firm, soft breasts and squeezed them hard. The combination of pain and pleasure set Janice off anew and she screamed as her pussy's messages of lust drove right to her brain.

When his eruptions ceased, the man's grip on Janice's breasts eased. Her own orgasmic pulses subsided. Exhausted, she lay her torso down on his. His chest was hot and covered with sweat from his exquisite ordeal. Janice reveled in the odor of his body and the pungent smell of her own arousal. Her breathing was deep and heavy as she sought recovery from her coital bout.

Tamarov stroked the girl's hair lightly. "She has crossed the line," he thought to himself. "Her lusts have been broken open, she has become a lustful whore." The experienced whoremaster was surprised that Janice had given herself over so quickly. She had only been a prisoner for three weeks. It probably felt more like three months to her. She had never been allowed to sleep for more than two or three hours. She had been fed small but nutritious meals six or seven times a day at varied intervals. Six weeks was the longest that any of the whores had held out. The system was infallible. The whole key was their 'voluntary' surrender to their fate. The fact that they had delivered themselves to their own damnation made them share in the guilt of their conversion from free, independent women, to willing and lustful sexual servants. "Mr. Kuribashi will be pleased," he thought.

But he wasn't done with the whore yet. Her fate was to live a life under the lash, to be subject to callous and stringent discipline. It would not due for her to think that throwing a good fuck raised her status. Her personality needed to be entirely broken.

The hard taskmaster pushed the young comfort girl off of him. "Assume your position, Number Four," he told her.

Janice, startled at the man's voice and his rude action, scrambled to her obey. She placed her hands behind her head and rose high on her knees, her back straight, her breasts pressed outwards. Tamarov rose slowly. He sat down next to the small table and poured himself a cup of tea. It was a pungent, black tea, redolent of the black soil of the Crimea where he had been born. Its bold taste pleased him and he savored it as it flowed down his throat.

"You have improved, Number Four," he told the anxious young woman. "But you still need much work. I think that we will double up on your punishments as a motivator. You will now receive ten lashes every training period. Five at the beginning and five at the end. Since this training period is coming to an end, I will administer your five strokes now."

Janice moaned when she heard the man's sentence pronounced on her. She hated the beatings more than anything. She would do anything to stop them. Tamarov was right when he assumed that the additional regimen of corporal punishment would motivate the girl to do better. She didn't now how, but she would convince them that she was the most obedient servant, the most lustful servant, the most obsequious slave. She swore it to herself even as she awaited the carrying out of Tamarov's cruel pronouncement.

The cruel Russian tossed back the rest of his tea. He stood. "Lean back until your shoulders touch the floor behind you, Number Four," he ordered in a low, curt voice.

There was no anger in it, no spite. It was just a command. One that was as compelling to the young girl as the need to breath.

Janice, keeping her hands dutifully locked on her head, moved her torso back slowly. Her back and thighs strained as her back came closer and closer to the floor. Tamarov had gone to the whip closet and by the time he turned around, a long, thin whip in his hand, Janice's shoulders were touching the mat behind her. Her body was shaking in anticipation of her upcoming ordeal. Her thigh muscles and her belly were stretched taut and her curved back ached. She realized that her breasts and belly were exposed to the man's trepidations. Just moments ago, she had been languishing in the bliss of the aftermath of powerful orgasms. But here she was, overwhelmed with terror. She was smart enough to know that she was being taught a lesson. She deserved no reward for bringing the man to exquisite pleasure. That was her job, what she was supposed to do. And it was her job to absorb whatever abuse her masters saw fit to inflict on her. She would take pain or pleasure as they saw fit.

"Now, Number Four," Tamarov told the supine woman, "I don't want to hear you screaming or yelling. It's time you developed better discipline than that. If you yell or scream, the stroke won't count and you'll just get another. Do you understand?"

A tear rolled down Janice's eye as she took in this new instruction. She didn't know if she could do it. But she knew that Tamarov would fulfill his threat without qualm if she disobeyed. "*Hai, Shukunsama!*" she replied loudly and brusquely as she had been taught, her voice strained and high pitched. She could feel her breasts tremble as her body shook with fear.

The cruel man raised the whip in his hand and brought it down swiftly onto the fragile and vulnerable, pale white breasts of the poor girl. The thin whip left a bright, red line across them. Janice pressed her lips tightly together and moaned with pain. But she did not call out her pain. "*Ichi!*" she called out loudly. "One!"

"Very good, Number Four," Tamarov observed calmly. He rose the whip up again and swung it fiercely forward, letting it strike the girl across her proffered belly. The lash was like a tongue of flame across Janice's midsection. "Ohhhhhhhh!" she cried in misery. But she kept her voice low, she bit her lip. She wanted to scream out to high heaven the injustice and callousness of the man's act. But she kept silent. She regained her composure and shouted out the Japanese word for the number two, "*Ni!*"

Smiling with self satisfaction, Tamarov readied the third blow. It struck across her stretched thighs. Again the girl gave out a moan of pain, but having fought back her need to shout out her suffering with all the effort she could muster, she yelled out "*San!*" The fourth blow landed next to the prior one on her stomach. "*Shi!*" the girl yelled frantically. She was sobbing now, her chest heaving. She knew that she was going to receive another kiss of the lash across her tender breasts. Her eyes were jammed shut. She bit her lip.

Tamarov took his time with the fifth and last lash of the whip. The tension in the room was palpable. He could hear the girl's heavy breaths, a small whine escaping her lips. "She is learning her lesson well," he thought to himself. "Good."

The fifth stroke was the hardest of the lot. A 'crack' resonated through the room as it made contact with the girl's flesh. It was too much for the girl. "Ohhhhhhhhh!"

she yelled out miserably. "Oh, god, please, no more, please!" she pleaded her tormentor. She realized that she had earned another stroke, but she could not hold in the pain from the lash's insult to her breasts.

"That's very bad, Number Four," the man said to her, his steely calm voice piercing her sobs. "I'll have to give you another, you know." He paused to let this sink in. "I'll let you prepare yourself for a moment."

He returned to the table and poured another small cup of the delicious tea. He picked up the fragile, hand painted cup and put it to his thin, cruel lips. He placed it down and returned to the girl. "Are you ready, Number Four," he asked her coldly.

"*Hai, Shukunsama*," she uttered forlornly.

"Well then," he told her, "here it comes."

He swung the whip over his head and gave the girl's breasts another stinging blow. This time Janice managed to suppress her urge to scream in pain. Her breasts were on fire, yet she managed to stifle all but a throaty moan.

"Very good, Number Four," Tamarov told her. "Now I want you to roll up the futon neatly while I get dressed."

Janice rolled over to her side and then raised herself to her knees. She scurried over to the futon and rolled it up tightly until it is pressed up against the wall. When she looked up, Tamarov was holding her gag. "Please put on your gag," Tamarov instructed her. Timidly, Janice took the leather belt with its long, thick plug and installed it on her face. She reached behind her head and buckled it in place.

"Stand up and turn around," the man ordered. He was fully dressed in neatly pressed, light gray slacks and a white polo shirt. He had black, leather sandals on his feet. Janice rose and turned. He gathered her arms and fastened her wrists together.

"Now get in your cage," she was told. In misery and self pity, Janice went to her knees and crawled to the steel enclosure. She shuffled herself into it and turned her torso, looking up at her master with dismay. He swung the cage door shut and locked it. "Enjoy your rest, Number Four. *Oyasumi nasai*," he told her. "Good night." He walked to the door and let himself out of the cell. A matron would come later to retrieve the small table. About five seconds after he shut the door, the room was plunged into darkness.

勢覇

CHAPTER SEVEN
PREPARATIONS

"Good evening."

"*Kon-ban wa.*"

"I am pleased to see you, sir."

"*Oaidekite kouei desu.*"

"I am very sorry, sir."

"*Moushiwake gozaimasen.*"

The voices of six exquisitely attractive, young women echoed in the small room. They were sitting cross-legged on the floor in a small circle, naked, their arms confined behind them. They all wore leather collars and bracelets around their wrists and ankles. They were repeating their lessons in Japanese for the day.

"May I serve you?"

"*Otetsudai shimashouka?*"

Janice struggled to pronounce the simple phrases. She knew that she had to get it right. Her trainer would ask her to repeat them later and she would be beaten for any mistakes.

It was five weeks since Janice had stepped into the fateful limousine and been driven to her present, unknown location. She tried not to think about what had been done to her, what her future might be. For here there was only the now, the immediate. Avoiding pain had become her watchword and the bruises and other evidence of her physical abuse on her body were testimony to her lack of success.

"What do you want to do?"

"*Dou shiyou ka?*"

Five expressions each day. Today's expressions were polite. Her last language session she had learned the expressions for "suck my cock", "spread your legs", and "present your ass", among others. She had been learning these expressions through trial and error from her trainer.

This was the fourth or fifth training session that Janice had had jointly with the other prisoners of the Budikan Corporation, she didn't really remember how many exactly. She had been surprised the first time that she had been led into the small room where the joint sessions were held. Ms. Yamamoto was leading it. "Come in, Number Four," she said politely when the matron had brought her through the door. "Please sit down."

There was a space between a stunning brunette and a beautiful black haired girl. Reluctantly, Janice drooped herself into the spot indicated. The matron removed her gag and left.

The room was slightly larger than the cell that she lived in, and the walls were decorated with large pen and ink Japanese prints. They seemed to be of a series and in each, the same man and woman were engaged in a variety of sexual acts and poses. The man was naked, but the woman was dressed in the traditional kimono of a geisha, her hair piled upon her head and thick with combs and picks. The loose, flowing fabric was pushed aside to reveal her naked flanks or pulled open to free her delicate breasts. Their genitals were clearly visible and grossly exaggerated. Janice took in the blatant sexuality of the prints while at the same time admiring the fineness of line, the clear demonstration of the couple's passion.

Rather than a rubberized mat like her cell, the floor was covered by a soft, peach colored rug. The walls were painted a soft pastel orange. The only furniture in the room was a small, oaken cabinet. Janice guessed accurately that the cabinet contained instruments of discipline and abuse.

"Let me introduce you to the other trainees," she continued once Janice got settled. She was wearing a bright yellow blouse and creased, tan slacks. Her feet were bare. There was a matron kneeling just behind and to the right of her.

"To your right is Number Five," the alluring woman said. "And to your left is Number Eight." Both girls bowed their heads respectfully as they were introduced. Like Janice, they wore their numbers hooked to the ring on the front of their collar. Janice bowed back as she had been taught.

"Across from you are Numbers, One, Three and Nine." Janice returned their respectful, if sullen bows. "We are beginning our language session for today. I will announce a phrase and the Japanese equivalent and the group will repeat it. After we go through the phrases a couple of times, I will say the English and the group will say the Japanese. Then we will have individual testing to see how much you have learned. I needn't remind you that this is a very important part of your education as a comfort girl. While many of our clients are not Japanese, almost all of the management positions in our company are. They will expect obedience to these simple commands and that you will be able to communicate with them on at least an elementary level. Comfort girls who do not meet the high standards of the Budikan Corporation put much shame on their trainers and are usually returned for corrective measures."

Ms. Yamamoto paused to let this information sink in. "Number Three has been returned for retraining and she has been subject to extreme discipline. Isn't that so, Number Three?"

Number Three was the beautiful, blond haired girl that Janice had seen the first day that she was here. Her head was covered by blond ringlets. Her body was a mass of red lines and deep black and blue marks. She had small, delicate breasts and long, thin nipples. Nervously, she answered the mistress in a subdued fearful voice, *"Hai, Yamamoto-san."*

Ms. Yamamoto led the bound women in a series of Japanese exercises. She had to correct Janice three times during the quiz phase. "You'll have to do a lot better, Number Four," she said. *"Tanakasama* will expect you to know these phrases by rote later in this training period. He will whip you very hard if you make any mistakes." And then to the small crowd of unhappy women, "Let's go through it one more time for the benefit of Number Four."

Janice strained to listen to the chorus of women to try and imprint in her memory the strange sounds she was required to know. She was aware of the truthfulness of Ms. Yamamoto's warning. Even though there were only five phrases, she felt that it was an impossible task. Her heart sunk when Ms. Yamamoto announced the termination of the exercise.

"Now that that is done, I would like Number Four to properly introduce herself," the woman announced. "Number Four, as you may have already surmised, there can be no sense of personal privacy or reticence about sexual matters for a comfort girl." She turned to the matron and gave her a whispered order in Japanese. The matron rose and knelt behind Janice releasing her bound wrists.

To Janice, the mistress said, "Number Four, you will spread your legs with your knees raised." To the others, she said, "Ladies, please form a semicircle so that you can all get a good view of Number Four's cunny."

Janice was mortified that these pretty, young women would be staring down at her nether lips. She watched as one by one they assumed a kneeling position in a rough semi circle about five feet away from her. Ms. Yamamoto took a position in their middle. Janice felt the matron kneel up against her back.

"Now, the matron will assist you, Number Four, but I want you to stroke yourself until you come. You needn't be bashful, all of the young ladies have done this and they won't be seeing anything new."

Ms. Yamamoto's eyes bore into Janice as she waited expectantly for the shocked girl to begin her task of self abuse. The matron had snuggled against her back so that Janice could use both her hands without falling backwards. She reached her arms around Janice's torso and began to tease the nipples of her breasts.

Janice hesitated. Here was yet another line for her to cross. She had performed this task many times in the privacy of her bed or in her bath, but never for someone else. And now she was to do it before a crowd of naked, staring women. She reached her hands down to her thighs and began to cry.

"Now, now, Number Four," Ms. Yamamoto said impatiently. "We'll have none of that. Whether you do it now or after a severe whipping is of no moment to me. You must rid yourself of these thoughts of sexual shame. They are not appropriate for a comfort girl."

"A comfort girl, a comfort girl," Janice thought miserably. "I don't want to be a comfort girl. I want to go home. I want to be left alone!" But she knew that Ms. Yamamoto again was speaking the truth. She would do it sooner or later. She would do anything to be spared the whip. She hated it, felt dirtied and shamed by her fear of it. Her hands crept slowly towards the 'vee' of her thighs. She felt the naked, hairless flesh of her plump labial lips. She felt the heat of the matron's body against her back. She felt the knowledgeable hands caressing her breasts. She closed her eyes and let her fingers explore the narrow opening between her protective lips. She let a finger slip between them and stroke their length. Her other hand began to rub the hood that hid her pleasure bud. "I'll pretend that they're not there," she thought to herself. "I'm all alone. I'm in my bed. There's music and the stillness of night."

The small crowd of trainees watched as Janice's sex began to moisten and distend. Her face, at first covered with fear and uncertainty, began to soften. She parted her lips and licked them nervously. But her hands kept at their tasks.

Janice felt her passion begin to rise. She had a vision of the other women watching her, saw her own hands stroking her sex, saw her own slit moistening and spreading open. The matron began to kiss her neck as she massaged her breasts. Janice pretended to be in the arms of a lover, that it was his hands stroking her. She let herself feel the tingling of her canal, the rush of pleasure as she stroked her now hard clit.

"Spread your legs wider, Number Four," Ms. Yamamoto said.

The unhappy girl was brought back to reality by the older woman's command. As she complied, she discovered that, in spite of her fears, she was finding something exciting about demonstrating her passion to all of these women. She opened her eyes to see their faces. Their eyes flitted between the actions of her hands, her breasts and her face. She saw the look of arousal in more than one visage. Ms. Yamamoto was staring at her with a most interested glare. She remembered the woman's hand on her pussy in her office, the way that she had expertly manipulated her to pleasure. She thought of the mouth of her matron, supping at the gate to her sex, her long, dexterous tongue dancing inside her. She imagined her trainer's prick filling her, driving her to ecstasy.

Her breath began to come heavy and she felt her lust building. When she had done this before, in her former life, she had always suppressed her climax, kept her passions tightly controlled. She had learned to liberate them since her recruitment as a comfort girl and she knew that they would flow freely now. Just the thought of her upcoming untrammeled release of lust made her sigh with anticipation.

She moaned and her eyes rolled back as the first waves of release ran through her. Her hands were working her pussy frantically. Her cunt began to pulse and throb and the pleasure made her abandon any scruples that may have remained about displaying herself in the throes of self induced pleasure. Her thighs quivered and her heart pounded heavily in her chest as the waves of pleasure flowed through her. The matron's hands massaged and caressed her breasts, urging her climax on and on. The young woman cried out as the sharp, intense contractions of her pussy shook her. She delved her fingers deeply inside herself as she relentlessly fingered her stiff, little pleasure nub.

Once her tremors had subsided, Janice, flushed and out of breath, opened her eyes to see the throng of female eyes staring at her. Lust was in their eyes as they appreciated the erotic display. Janice's hand was damp with her own moisture. She wiped it clean on her thigh.

"Very good, Number Four," Ms. Yamamoto said. "Now please give each of your sisters a very nice kiss."

Helped by the strong arms of the matron behind her, Janice rose to her knees and crawled over to the waiting women. The first was the one who wore the number eight attached to her collar. Her hair was long and jet black and she had thin, black eyebrows arched over her eyes. Her complexion was pale and her eyes were blue. She licked her lips as Janice approached her and opened her mouth when the still lust filled girl brought her lips to hers. Janice pressed her lips against the lips of the pretty, black haired girl. They were warm and soft. She pulled back as swiftly as she could.

"No, no, Number Four," Ms. Yamamoto protested. "A real kiss, like you meant it."

Hesitatingly, Janice brought her lips back to bear on the soft lips of Number Eight. She sensed a smile on the opening lips. When their lips joined, Janice felt her tongue sucked in by the pretty girl. The girl's hands were still imprisoned behind her and she leaned her torso against Janice's to maximize their physical contact. Her breasts were firm and high on her chest. Janice felt them pressed against hers and her lust began to build again. She placed her hands on the thin hips of Number Eight and drank of her mouth's heat. Her hand wandered to the girl's chest and she gently held her hard breast in her hand. She didn't know what she was doing; she was in a haze of lust. She released the black haired girl and approached the next,

Number Five, who had large, soft breasts and thick, plump lips. Her chestnut colored hair was shoulder length and her eyes brown. Janice drew a deep breath before their lips joined. She circled her arm around the girl's back and drew her into herself while pushing her tongue deep into the hungry mouth. Her pussy burned as electricity passed between them.

One by one, Janice kissed all of the pretty girls. She felt their breasts, their thighs and their taut bellies. She pressed herself against them, needing their heat. When she had kissed them all, including the poor, unhappy Number Three, with all of her bruises and welts, she presented herself to Ms. Yamamoto.

"That's all for today, ladies," Ms Yamamoto announced. "Number Four, please pick up you co-workers' gags and put them back in. I'll signal for the matrons."

The comfort girls' gags were in a little pile by the door. Each one had a small tag with the owner's number on it. Janice picked them up and moved to each girl one at a time and slid the thick, leather plug inside the appropriate yawning mouth. She looked carefully into the eyes of each girl as she did so. She was met with a series of forlorn, unhappy glances. They were prisoners like her. Had they surrendered themselves to the power of the Budikan Corporation like she had? Each girl was, in her own way, a desirable, sensuous woman. Was she looking at a reflection of herself, she thought. Was her body as smooth and her breasts as delectable as theirs? They kneeled erect when Janice presented their gags to their mouths. Her breasts rubbed against theirs as she placed her arms over their shoulders to attaché the gags at the back of their heads. Her loins remembered the passion she had felt as she had kissed each one of their lips. She was surprised that she had felt lust at another woman's lips, never mind so many. What had she been missing?

When she approached Number Three, the unfortunate blond haired girl, she sensed a special feeling of fear and misery within her. Janice knew how cruel and exacting her trainer and the others were with her. How much worse could it be for a girl who was returned because of unacceptable performance of her duties? Janice wondered where the girl had been. What was it like to serve as a comfort girl? Was there any relief from the dehumanizing treatment she had suffered since her own transmutation? Did life have any joys? She yearned to speak to the forlorn, young woman. Her blue eyes teared as the gag went home. Undoubtedly, her trainer awaited her. This session with the mistress must have seemed like heaven.

Janice knelt before the tall, thin lady as several matrons came in to lead the young women either back to their cells, to the baths or to another training session. She awaited the instruction to reapply her own gag. But the woman waited until all the other girls had left before speaking to her. Janice's sex still tingled with the afterglow of her passage 'around the horn', so to speak. Ms. Yamamoto smiled at the young girl. "You haven't kissed me yet, Number Four," she observed. "Bring me your lips."

Janice made a sidelong look at the matron who had resumed her place behind and to the right of her mistress. Janice crawled over to the kneeling Eurasian woman, her mistress. The woman's arms greeted her as she leaned over to join their lips together. She felt a deep, tense pull on her sex as her tongue found the older woman's. Ms. Yamamoto's arms circled around her and she pulled her body in against hers. Unconsciously, Janice's arms wrapped around her mistress's torso and she returned the passionate embrace. Her legs were spread and Ms. Yamamoto's knees were inside her own. She pressed her thighs against them in her need. Her mind swooned as she absorbed the lust of the tall, svelte woman.

Ms. Yamamoto released the impassioned comfort girl and pushed her away. Her long, black hair had been wrapped into a bun upon her head and she reached up and loosened it, letting it fall to her shoulders and down her back. Her hands came to her blouse and slowly, but surely, unbuttoned it until it fell open, revealing a fine, lacy bra supporting her small, round breasts.

"Some of your clients may be women, Number Four," Ms. Yamamoto told Janice as she reached behind her to loosen her bra, "and it is important that you learn how to please a woman. Besides, you are a beautiful, young thing, and I have been waiting patiently for the opportunity to sample you."

The woman stood and drew her slacks down her long, lithe legs. She was wearing a pair of thin, silk, white panties and the black hair of her trimmed sex stood out as a shadow behind them. Without fanfare, she slid the panties down off of her legs and tossed them aside. She got down on her knees before the younger woman.

Janice was taken aback by the woman's beautiful body. When their lips joined again, she drew in her wonderful scent as her hot flesh rubbed against her. Ms. Yamamoto pulled her to her side until they were both lying on their sides on the floor. Her tongue slid over and under and around Janice's in a passionate gambol. She pressed the length of her body against Janice's and threw her thigh over Janice's hip. The young girl could not get enough of her mistress's heat. One arm locked beneath her, she wrapped the other around the woman's long, languorous back and reveled in the smooth skin underneath her fingers.

Gently, Ms. Yamamoto pushed Janice to her back. She covered her body with her own and pulled her arms high over her head, stretching them out in a wide 'vee'. She pushed her thighs in between the comfort girl's and urged them apart. Janice could feel the top of the woman's mound brush against hers. The woman began to grind her hips, drawing her hairy mons along Janice's dilated slit. She found the young woman's mouth once more and their lips locked together in lust.

Nothing had prepared Janice for this experience. She felt like she was being devoured by the older, taller woman. Ms. Yamamoto was all of 27 years old, but the gap in their ages seemed trebled by the other woman's power and experience. Again and again, Ms. Yamamoto drew her sex against Janice's. Janice felt her heat building higher and higher. Her body began to squirm beneath the older woman's. Ms. Yamamoto felt it and broke their kiss to whisper into Janice's ear. "Not, yet, little comfort girl, not yet. Hold on till I tell you."

Obedient to her mistress's command, subservient to her lover's wishes, Janice fought to hold her passions from cresting. She moaned as Ms. Yamamoto's tongue found hers again. Their breasts rubbed together as their torsos writhed passionately. Harder and harder, Ms. Yamamoto ground her hips against Janice's. Finally, the woman moaned into Janice's mouth. "Now!" she commanded. "Now!"

Janice felt the dam of her passions burst and her empty vault clenched hard on itself. She groaned and shouted out her pleasure as wave after wave of ecstasy poured through her. The mistress was riding her hard, pushing the apex of her sex hard against Janice's stiff button. She bit Janice's neck sharply, causing the young woman to scream with pleasure and pain. "Ohhhhhhhhh!" she yelled. "Yes! Yes!" she called out, pushing her hips hard against the other woman's. "Oh, god! Oh! Oh! Oh!"

The women's bodies came to rest against each other's, their forces exhausted. After regaining her breath, Ms. Yamamoto drew her lips along Janice's neck and chin and then gave her one last, passionate kiss. Her hair fell around her face like a black curtain. She raised her head above the younger woman's. "In our next session, Number Four, you'll learn to please a woman with your mouth." She slid her body off of Janice's and, reaching down, gathered her pussy's moisture on her fingers. She presented it to the young whore's mouth.

"Lick my hand clean, Number Four. Learn to like the taste of a woman's cum."

Janice took the woman's fingers in her mouth and cleaned them of her liquids. The taste was strange to her, the smell pungent.

"And one day, soon, before you leave us, I'll come to your cell and beat you so I can hear you scream."

Janice shivered at the woman's harsh promise. She looked into her dark, almost black eyes and saw the icy cruelty there. But she said that she would be leaving soon. Where would she go? Who would she serve and where? She remembered the globe from the video with all the little flags on it. It could be anywhere, it could be anyone. Her life was truly lost.

Ms. Yamamoto had Janice kneel in the middle of the room with her hands on her head while she dressed. She ordered the matron to restore her gag. She patted Janice on the cheek and smiled at her before she left. The trainee comfort girl remained there, still, filled with trepidation and fear for the future, until an hour later when her matron came to get her.

* * * * * * * * * * * *

And so the sessions with the mistress continued. Not all of the same girls were there each time. As far as Janice could tell, the numbers went up to ten. Sometimes, the session involved only two or three girls; the most she ever saw assembled was six. Janice wondered about these other girls. They were pretty and willing. They carried marks of their abuse as she did. Their passions seemed real when invited to the center of the group to bring themselves off or to pleasure another trainee. At the end of every session, one of them remained behind for the pleasure of the Mistress.

Janice never saw the unfortunate Number Three again. On one occasion, there was a new Number Five. Janice assumed that the old one had been sent on to her first assignment as a comfort girl. The new girl was a hazel eyed beauty, with long, graceful legs and dark, Mediterranean skin. As had Janice, the girl was forced to pleasure herself for the entertainment of the others. She broke down half way through and had to be whipped. The next training session, she completed her task without further ado.

True to her promise, the mistress had Janice learn the art of cunnilingus. Her first lesson occurred in front of her 'sister' trainees. She was instructed to "do what comes natural," and she performed her task without hesitation and with alacrity. She was surprised at how much the taste and aroma of the other young woman's sex aroused her. And when the girl began to moan and twist with pleasure,

Janice's tongue buried deep in her quim, Janice felt a thrill in her own loins.

Her training was stepped up in other areas as well. She was taken to the trainers' meal room where she was taught how to serve her masters. A bright, cheery Japanese girl dressed in a modest frock taught her how she would be required to make up her face and her body, and giggled girlishly when she administered rouge to Janice's already dark areolas and perfume to the crevice between her thighs. She learned how to pleasure a man in the company of another woman, both of them applying their hard won skills on him at the same time.

And the tall, gray haired man came to see her regularly. Often, he would whip her for his own pleasure. Sometimes he would administer the strokes that she was due as part of her training regimen.

It was during this period that Janice began to service some of the junior executives of the company. There were more than eighty in the building, most of them on temporary assignment away from Japan. That they would need an outlet for their sexual passions was considered quite normal. They would enter Janice's little cell dressed in their short sleeve whit, poplin shirts and ties. Janice, naked, would pour them tea and remove their clothes. Although servicing the company men was rather undemanding, Janice hated it with a passion. Each time, when the men dressed and left her, she would cry. She was now officially a whore. There was no pretense of social interaction between her and the men. None of them asked her her name; most barely spoke to her. But all of them thanked her with a polite bow when they were finished with her.

Janice was becoming anxious to be 'promoted' from the dreadful confines of the training floor. She had not seen the sun shine for a long time. It was as if the rest of the world did not exist for her. She wondered, from time to time, where the trainers and the matrons and Ms. Yamamoto went when their shifts were over. Did they have real lives? Children? Did they go to the movies? Restaurants? It seemed to Janice that her matron was almost always there. Were the matrons prisoners too?

One 'morning' (Janice didn't really know what time it was, but she counted each commencement of a training period, marked by five lashes of the whip, as a 'morning'), a strange Asian man came into her cell. He was carrying a bag of equipment and an unusual chair. He bowed formally to Janice, stepped up and confirmed her tag number on her collar. He then motioned for her to sit in the chair, which he had placed in the center of the room.

When Janice sat in the small, wooden chair, she found herself leaning back at a 90 degree angle to the floor. The man, wearing black pants and a white barber's jacket, lifted Janice's thighs and attached them to planks that came out on either side of the chair. As a result, Janice's legs were spread wide. The delicate inside of her thighs were exposed as well as her naked nether lips.

The girl was somewhat disconcerted at the man's treatment of her. Nothing here happened without a reason and, she figured, there must be some sinister intent in requiring her to submit to the chair's demands. The Asian man, short with black hair and glasses, fastened each of Janice's hands to the chair's sides and drew a strap around her chest, just below her breasts. He then sat back and fished something out of his bag. Janice recognized it immediately. It was a tattoo gun. She was going to be tattooed!

The comfort girl was still wearing her gag and so could not vocalize her protestations. She did whine with misery as she saw the man hooking jet black ink up to the needle. She cried and began to struggle when she heard the instrument buzz to life.

The man sat back on his heels and frowned at Janice's lack of compliance. He reached back into his little black bag and pulled out a box containing a set of long needles. He paused, selected one, and put the box back in the bag. He showed it to Janet and then leaned over an addressed it to the slit between her thighs.

The poor girl was frantic. She had no idea what he was going to do with the needle, but she knew that it would be to her detriment. Using one hand to guide him, the man carefully inserted the needle at the base of Janet's pleasure bud. At first, there was no reaction other than the strangeness of having an implement driven into her body. The man pulled the needle out and then tried again. This time, when the needle had been inserted no more than an inch and a half, Janice experienced an explosion of pain. The man, clearly well versed in female anatomy had found the root of a nerve. Janice moaned in pain and tried to hop out of the little chair. The man jiggled the needle and wave after wave of excruciating torment went through her. Finally, he sat back, leaving the needle in place and just smiled. After a moment, he returned his hand to the needle and touched it with a finger. The slight movement of the needle made Janice sweat with agony. The slight, black haired man looked Janice in the eyes again and renewed his smile. He didn't say a word, but Janice knew his message. She would remain perfectly still.

Going back to his task, the man began to apply the tattooing needle to an area on the inside of Janice's right thigh, no more than an inch away from the crease of where her loins met her leg. It hurt to have that tender skin pricked, but it was not as bad as the needle stuck below her clit and so Janice peaceably accepted whatever mark the man was putting on her.

After about a half hour, the man finished with the right thigh and started on the left. Another half an hour and he was done with that one too. Janice was in despair. Although from her leaning back position, she had not seen the tattoos, she realized that she had probably just been marked as property of the Budikan Corporation. It brought home to her the desperate nature of her plight. No one knew where she was. The police had been corrupted and would probably have erased all records of her complaints. Even her former employer seemed to be in on it, reporting her for having stolen money. And then, if she could somehow get away from these people, where could she go? What would she do? She would have to live a life on the run. Maybe she could go to the FBI? But if somehow they were corrupted too and she had to be brought back here for 'retraining', she was sure that her fate would be much more severe then the blond girl's, who had only "failed to perform her duties adequately".

Janice wondered what the man had tattooed on her body. She feared that it was something obscene like 'whore' or 'slut'. She hadn't seen any tattoos on the other girls, but maybe it was something that they gave you just before you were 'graduated' to official duties. She had not seen anything on the blond girl, Number Three, but then the girl had not had her legs spread and Janice had been only been able to giver her cursory attention.

The man packed up his things. Before removing the long pin he had inserted in Janice's sex, he gave it one more juggle. Janice closed her eyes and moaned as the pain paralyzed her. The man kept moving the infernal pin for about ten seconds, long agonizing seconds for the tattooed comfort girl.

When he was done, and had finished putting away his things, he got to his feet and bowed to the grotesquely displayed girl. "*Arigatou gozaimasu, Nanba-shi,*" he told her. "Thank you, Number Four." Janice, gagged, did not reply. He left her sitting in the chair, bound to it, when he left the room.

Janice desperately yearned to learn what he had inscribed on her thighs. She realized that anyone who spread her thighs to gain access to her sex would see it. Every time she opened her legs she would think of it. An hour later, the matron entered. She undid Janice's gag and gave her something to drink. She held a small bedpan under her sex so that she could pee. Janice wanted to ask the woman to show her the tattoos, but she was afraid to speak to her. She had been whipped on every occasion that she initiated a conversation.

As if she had read Number Four's mind, the matron dragged the little chair over to the front wall of the cell and turned the chair around so that she had a full view of the room. Since her make-up training had started, Janice had a mirror in the room so that she could learn to apply the facial and body decorations herself. Every time she saw her face in the mirror applying the emblems of her degradation, she cursed herself as a wanton, sluttish whore.

The matron took the wide, tall mirror and propped it up in front of the girl. She raised the back of the chair slightly so that Janice could look at her own loins. There, clearly imprinted on the inside of each thigh were the ideograms representing the Budikan Corporation. Janice sobbed as she realized the significance of the markings. She was their property. Her body, her will, her mind, belonged to them. And everyone who used her would know it.

Although the symbols were backwards in the mirror, Janice recognized them right away. They had been part of her everyday life for as long as she had been a prisoner, inscribed in tall, thick lines on the walls of her cell. She had often looked at them while ensconced in her cage, wondering at their meaning, hating their very existence. They made her feel small, insignificant, over powered.

The matron leaned over from Janice's side and pointed to the ideogram etched into her left thigh. "Strength," she said in explanation. She pointed to the other. "Dominance," she said. "Very powerful. You little girl, no power. Budikan Corporation, much power. You are comfort girl. Obey, give pleasure. Understand?"

It was the most that the matron had ever spoken to her. With tears flowing down her face, Janice nodded her understanding. She was a small, powerless whore, worse than a whore.

Janice was still crying when the matron reinserted her gag. The woman produced a chain with a clip on the end and fastened it to the ring on the shield attached to the thick, leather plug. She pulled it tight and attached it to a ring in the center of the chair, between Janice's legs. The girl's head was forced down and, if she kept her eyes opened, she would be greeted by the vision of her splayed legs and the insidious markings at their tops. The matron bowed to the girl and left the room.

For twelve hours, Janice was forced to sit and gaze into the mirror at the signs of her own enslavement. She was allowed out of the chair only to eat and to use the chamber pot. At times, she sat their listlessly, numbed by the reality of what she had become. At others, she raged and cursed her masters, herself, her deity. And at others, laughing, almost delirious, she stared intently at her own proffered naked and hairless slit. She realized, ironically, that, braced by the two evil ideograms, there lay the instrument of her own strength and power. The need and hunger for her cunt was a form of domination. She would use it thusly. She would make them mad with desire for it and for the use of her other orifices. She was a comfort girl. Only she and her sisters could provide the comfort for these men's terrible needs. They could beat her, cage her, defile her, but, in the end, they would use her to quench their desperate fires.

勢霸

CHAPTER EIGHT
SELECTION

After the wounds of her tattoos had healed, it seemed to Janice that everyone wanted to come and take a look at them. She felt humiliated and ashamed every time one of them, be it one of the trainers or Tamarov, made her spread her legs to show them off. Invariably, they would finish by pushing her legs back and entering her from the front, their faces grinning at hers. There was something about the feeling of being owned and marked that made Janice feel that she somehow had done something to deserve all the cruelty and abuse she had suffered for who knows how long. If she had felt that she was becoming a whore and a slut, this was proof positive.

The idea that she had been 'smoked out' from her prior restrained, if not totally chaste' sexual habits, gave Janice the license to toss aside any reservations she may have still had about submerging herself into the sea of sexual experience she had been tossed into. Or rather, had dove into. For she constantly remembered that it was her own volitional efforts that had brought her here. She had made the telephone call, she had agreed to apply, she had gotten into the limousine. Sure, she had been forced by circumstances, but she could have made them drag her out of apartment kicking and struggling. Then, all would have been imposed on her by others. But as it was, she felt that she had been weak, submissive, a coward.

The reappearance of the large, callous, Asian man who had tormented her in her own apartment brought all of that back to her. She was kneeling in the center of the room, her hands behind her head, in obedience to the blue light when he walked in. Immediately as she saw him, her stomach dropped and she began to sweat with fear. She remembered how roughly he had handled her in her apartment when his activities were somewhat circumscribed by the fact that it took place in a fully occupied apartment building. But here, no one would respond to her screams of torment. There was no restriction on the manner or duration of her use.

The Asian man was wearing the kimono of a trainer, green and red, and it looked like a whole bolt of cloth had to be used to cover his massive frame. Behind him were two matrons carrying small tables, one of which had placed on it three covered bowls of food and the other a small pitcher of sake and a delicate porcelain cup. He was carrying what looked like a large skein of coarse rope.

The matrons scurried from the room and Janice was alone with the Korean. Nangi Shikata came from a long tradition of Korean gangsters. His father had been an enforcer for the South Korean secret police for many years. And before that, his grandfather had worked for the Japanese occupiers. They all worked dutifully and loyally for their masters, in his grandfather's case, to the death, as he was butchered by Korean guerillas when the Japanese were forced to leave the Korean peninsula after World War Two. But for him and his forbears, the rest of the world consisted of pawns to be played with, used, terminated, as they saw fit or as they were ordered to do. As he poured himself a cup of sake and looked at the forlorn beauty kneeling before him he saw only a source of potential sexual and sadistic satisfaction. She was pretty, yes. Desirable, yes. But that's what made it so much fun.

Nangi tossed back the contents of the tiny cup and began to unfurl the rope. There was a ring in the ceiling in the center of the room, and Janice had been whipped many times with her hands tied to it above her head. She quailed at the thought of him whipping her. She was perplexed when she saw him draw out an arm length or two of the rope and then tie her ankles together, crossing them. He then grabbed her arms and joined them behind her back. Crossing in front of the frightened girl, he knelt in front of her. He grabbed her cheeks with his large, right hand and squeezed until Janice opened her mouth.

She did not resist him, but the force of his grasp hurt her all the same. Nangi put his face close to hers and thrust his thick tongue into her mouth. He swirled it inside over her tongue, underneath and against the sides of her oral cavity. His other hand was on her right breast, pinching it hard with his mighty paw. Janice squirmed and whined as she was overwhelmed with pain and revulsion at his rape of her mouth. It felt to her like an oily leech had entered it. The fat, tall Asian then withdrew his tongue from her mouth and used it to lap his saliva all up and down her face. Janice tried to move her head away, but he had slid his right hand down under her chin and held her head firmly in place. When he was done wetting her cheeks and forehead, and even her eyelids, with his gross muscle, he pulled back and laughed.

He circled the rope around Janice's torso just under her breasts and tied it off on her left side. There still considerable rope left in his hand from the long strand. He circled Janice's right breast with the rope and tied it off tightly, until Janice felt her breast harden with entrapped blood. He then did the same to the other breast. The rope was then taken around her chest over her breasts twice and once more under them. He tied a knot in the back pinching all of the parts of the rope together and then ran the end through the gap between her locked arms.

Janice was startled when the huge man then pushed her so that she was face down on the mat. The ropes were itchy and coarse and tied uncomfortably tight. Janice sensed the man doing something with the ring in the ceiling and then she felt the two ends of the rope, the end connected to her ankles and the end tied off behind her back start to tense. The Korean gave a mighty heave and the rope pulled the unfortunate girl right up off of the floor. Janice moaned with discomfort as her legs and torso were forced into a crescent. Her back ached at the strain. She remembered how the man had tied her up in her apartment and shivered when she thought of how he was unrestrained in his use of her here.

Nangi pulled on the two ends of the rope until Janice's body was about three feet off of the ground. As she whined in pain, he took the two ends of the rope and, raising her arms behind her as high as they would go, tied them off around the joinder of the girl's wrists. Janice was now suspended from three points. Her back and shoulders hurt from the strain that her weight put on them. The pain from her arms being raised up behind her was agonizing. "Ohhhhhhhhh!" she moaned in pain as she realized that it was probably the man's intent to leave her this way for some time. She wanted to beg him to release her, but she was too frightened of what he would do if she spoke out of turn. She found that she could lessen the strain on her upraised arms by trying to straighten out her body so that more weight was taken up by the ropes connected to her chest and ankles. But she could only tense her body like that 15 or 20 seconds at a time before her hips started to suffer.

The cruel Korean went over to the cabinet that housed a chamber of horrors and removed a thick leather ring gag. He came back to Janice and jammed it in her mouth. She let out a garbled, "Gaaaaa!" as he forced it in, distending her jaw and her lips. Tears were flowing down her face which was just at the level of his loins when he stood before her. She knew what he was going to do to her. She just prayed that he would do it quickly, get it over with, and release her.

But that was not what the large man intended. He had been taught patience and to savor his sensual enjoyments. And right now, he intended to enjoy the girl's distress while eating his meal and drinking some sake. There was a long, thick, leather plug that fit inside the leather covered steel ring in the girl's mouth and he jammed it in, clipping its sides to two small tabs on the ring. Janice groaned as she realized that her abysmal state was to be prolonged. She looked up at the man pleadingly and issued a long, piteous whine, muffled by the thick leather in her mouth.

The big Korean sat down cross legged in front of the hapless young woman. He picked up one of the bowls from the table and unlidded it. A small cloud of steam arose and he savored it with his nose. He picked up the pair of black and gold lacquered chop sticks from the table and commenced to eat.

While eating, the man kept his eyes on the spectacle of the dangling woman. He enjoyed hearing her moan. The room was small and her head was about two feet away from him. While masticating a piece of especially succulent steamed eel, he placed his hand on Janice's face and gave her a small shove. Her body swung back and forth as a result, adding to the already intolerable pain in her back, legs and arms. "Ooooooooooo!" she moaned as her body coursed backwards and forwards. The man seemed to enjoy his little joke and he pushed her again harder. "Oh! Oh! Oh!" she called out, her voice muffled, her eyes communicating her plea for mercy. The Korean laughed and resumed eating.

When he picked up the third bowl, after having downed several shots of the fierce liquor, the man took a sample in his mouth and closed his eyes to savor it. When he opened them, he seemed to remember something. His eyes lit up and a look of merriment crossed his face. He put down his chopsticks and the bowl and leaned over, removing the thick gag that he had shoved inside the leather covered steel ring in Janice's mouth. Janice had been softly moaning, her eyes also shut, trying to think away what had subsided into dull, throbbing aches. She was startled when she felt the gag being removed and when she opened her eyes she saw the gleeful face of the Asian man. He picked up the bowl of food and took out a small piece of chicken. As soon as Janice saw it, she realized what he was going to do. "Eeeeeease own't!" she tried to say miserably. "Eeeease!"

Chuckling, Nangi took the steaming piece of chicken and dropped it into Janice's mouth through the hole in the ring gag. Janice tried to push it out with her tongue, but only managed to get it lodged underneath. It took about three seconds for the flaming hot spices to spread throughout her mouth.

"Auwhhhhh! Auwhhhhhhh!" she cried as her mouth alit with harsh reaction to the hot spices. "Auwwwwwh! Eeease on't!"

Nangi was beside himself. He laughed so hard that his eyes began to tear. He remembered this little girl and the fun he had with her in her kitchen. He had wanted to fuck her then, but that was against the rules. Not that he was afraid anyone would do anything to him, but, after all, rules were rules. But now, she was his to do what he wanted.

He reached into her mouth with the chopsticks and retrieved the meat. He didn't want to have her choke. He chewed the piece and swallowed it quickly. He took another piece from the bowl. He held it up for the girl to see, tauntingly. Janice struggled in her bonds, an activity that only made them tighter and caused her more pain. When the man moved the meat closer to her mouth, she tied to fight it off with her tongue. But it was no match for Nangi's insistence and she felt the chicken being swabbed against her tongue, along the sides of her mouth and to the edge of her throat. The same fire arose and she screamed for mercy once again. Nangi removed it after coating it with her mouth's juices and swallowed it, laughing.

When he had finished the bowl, after dipping each seriously spicy piece inside the girl's mouth, to her consternation and dismay, Nangi took three consecutive gulps of sake. He shook his head after the third one, relishing the rush. Janice was in misery. Her mouth burned from the huge man's little game. As she sensed him rising to his feet, she knew that her time to perform had come.

Nangi squatted before the girl, his face inches from hers. For a second, she was afraid that he was going to bite off her nose. But instead, he reached under the bowed woman and seized her dangling breasts with both hands.

Janice shuddered when she felt his hands on her hard, swollen globes. They had been aching for about twenty minutes, as long as she had been hanging at the Asian man's mercy. When he squeezed them, they felt like they were likely to pop. She moaned in pain again. He took hold of the nipples and twisted them harshly. Janice cried out with the pain.

Satisfied at the discomfort of the girl, his cock now having grown to hardness, and prompted by the woman's verbal expressions of torment, he stood and presented the tip of his meat to the middle of the ring gag. His cock was not long, but it was very thick and filled the whole gap between Janice's lips. His manhood crushed her tongue against the bottom of her mouth and scraped along its top and the top of her mouth. Her nerve endings were still sensitive from the spicy food and Janice moaned in discomfort. She felt him grab her braided hair behind her head and begin to stroke her head back and forth on his steel like rod. Janice groaned with pain as her muscles were strained by the involuntary movement. "Ga...ga...ga...ga!" she uttered as his fat cock repeatedly struck the edge of her throat.

Nangi's cock was rock hard and his body was thrusting forwards to match the movement of his hand and Janice's head. "Mmmmmmmmmmmm!" he sighed with delight. He could hear the unwilling exclamations of the girl each time he struck her throat. "This is how it should be," he thought. He looked down to see her straining hands, her arched back, her twisted ankles. Her exclamations were music to his ears.

When his crises came, he drew his cock back so just the head of it stood inside the girl's mouth. His hand circled his meat and he began to pump it furiously. His jism jetted out wildly into Janice's mouth and onto her tongue. It came too fast for her to swallow it all and it started to fill up her mouth. "Awwwwgh!" she exclaimed as she feared to choke to death on the man's spunk. But his throbbing spasms began to recede and the flow of sticky, salty substance finally diminished.

While his prick was still hard, the satisfied man slid it back home within Janice's mouth and savored her moist warmth while it detumesced. With her mouth held wide open by the ring gag, Janice had a very limited ability to swallow the Asian's spunk and when the man finally exited her, it still lay fallow within. Janice felt it dribble down her chin as her mouth refilled with saliva.

Nangi had drunk all of the sake from his carafe. There was a speaker by the door, used by the trainers and others when they needed or wanted to communicate with the outside, and the man issued a curt order through it. While he was waiting, he picked off of the wall a long, skinny, leather whip that was hanging there for the convenience of Janice's trainers. When Janice heard him swishing it through the air, her heart began to pound. She expected nothing but the most vicious cruelty from this behemoth of a man. Nangi looked her over and decided that the upturned soles of her bound feet were an appropriate target.

Janice felt the fire cross the bottom of her left foot and howled. The ring gag was still in her mouth and her exclamation emerged as a kind of "Ooooooool!" Nangi looked at the product of his effort. He was satisfied to see a line of red emerge immediately. He reared back and struck the other foot. Janice howled again. He decided that he liked the sound of her hollering through the hole in her gag and he struck her six times in a quick, measured cadence. Janice's voice lowed through out the room in a steady stream. She wanted to try and beg him to stop, but she couldn't catch her breath to make even a distorted supplication. Nangi had raised the whip for another stinging blow when the door to the cell opened and a matron brought in another quart carafe of hot sake.

The arrival of his liquid sustenance gave the cruel man pause. To Janice's relief, he tossed the whip aside and grabbed the bottle from the frightened matron. She backed out of the room bowing and thanking the fearsome man for his courtesy in accepting her gift.

Nangi immediately poured himself a cup of the hot refreshment and threw it to the back of his throat. Then he did another, and another. Placing the cup on the table, he looked over the form of his suspended victim. Her face was awash with tears and her eyes peered up at him with terror. He gave her head a little shove and watched her swing back and forth. He decided that his arrangement of the whore had served its purpose and proceeded to release the ropes around her wrists and lower her to the floor.

Janice moaned with relief as her body touched ground and the pressure on her shoulders and back subsided. She gave a loud groan as her back straightened. Nangi quickly undid the ropes around her body, rolling her torso this way and that to get them off of her. Janice yelled in pain when the ropes around her breasts were released, but was grateful all the same. She lay there limply on her belly as the man went and got another drink.

The whip that Nangi had discarded was within his arms reach and he leaned over and retrieved it. He looked at the still suffering female with disdain and he lashed out with the whip across her buttocks. Janice was taken by surprise by the blow and Squealed "Oooooooo!" through her gag.

"Kneel, slut!" the deep voiced man yelled at her. Immediately, fearful of the consequences of anything but the most alacrative response, Janice rose to her knees.

"Come here," he growled at her.

Dismally unhappy, her arms still bound behind her, Janice edged herself over to proximity with the beastly man. He reached out and, grabbing her nipples in his hands, drew her closer. He snaked one huge arm around her waist and underneath her bound arms and fastened his big, sloppy lips on her teat. His mouth covered the top third of Janice's ample breasts and he suckled on her, drawing her nipple deeply into his mouth, running his tongue over it and then nipping at it with his teeth. After all of the pain he had inflicted on her, his ministrations to her breast felt like heaven to the unfortunate young woman. He shifted breasts and Janice began to feel her nipples tighten and her slit to moisten. Her knees were spread wide apart and Nangi was able to insinuate his large hand between them and capture the girl's sex with it.

Janice expected the man to impose some brutality on her vulnerable pussy lips, but, instead, she felt him begin to stroke the tender organ gently. He continued his attention to her breasts, licking wide circle around her areolas, flicking his tongue over the tips of her nipples, while he delved his fingers deeper and deeper into the girl's dilating tunnel.

It was surreal to Janice to be now experiencing the nascent delirium of pleasure after so much abuse. But she had learned to adapt and to welcome pleasure whatever its source and whenever it came. Nangi's fingers teased the little nub at the apex of her loins, spreading her moisture over it. Janice sighed as his fat fingers entered her again.

Within a short time, Janice began to feel the building of her lusts. Her breathing became deep and her breasts hard. Nangi took note and leaned back while he continued his manipulation of her sex. He examined her face closely as she began to pant with passion. Janice looked into his empty eyes and saw his cruelty there. This delivery of delightful sensations was not for her benefit. It was to amuse the man, to exhibit his power over her body. But Janice didn't care. Her lusts had gone too far for that and she began to rock her hips as the hand drove her closer and closer to completion.

"Aooooo! Aooooo!" she moaned from her grossly distended mouth, through the hole in her gag, as she felt her fires alight. Her hands twisted behind her. Her body shook as she came and she called out, "Gaaaaaa! Gaaaaaaaa!" as her pussy's spasms tore through her. The man was smiling at her, satisfied at her reaction. His smile was somewhat lopsided, his face somewhat droopy from the booze, but he knew what he was about and he continued to stroke and pet the girl's cunt until she called out again, "Gaaaaaa! Gaaaaaa!"

Without ado, the man shoved Janice over to her side and then turned her, forcing her back to him. He pushed her torso down until she was bent over her knees. Janice felt his hands on the outside of her thighs and his thick, hard meat address the portal to her womb. When he slid in, the sensation of his hot mass filling her made her gasp.

Although the man's gut was huge, he was able to pierce Janice's canal to the hilt. His large hands covered both of her rear cheeks as he plowed her dripping furrow. Janice had been already on the boil and his attentions to her pussy made her wild with lust. She thrust back at the man's cock, looking for its rasp across her hard button. "Aaaah!

Aaaaaaah! Aaaaaaaaaah!" she called out as her pussy's convulsions began again. She felt the man stiffen and his hot discharge within her. His muscle flexed and throbbed within her as she buried her face on the soft mat beneath her and screamed.

When his pulsing cock came to rest, Nangi slid it from Janice's soaking crevasse and pushed her over. He sat back and poured himself another sake. Janice was trying to recover her breath when she heard him yell, "Kneel!" She quickly regained her knees and faced her assailant.

"What will he do next?" she wondered fearfully as she watched him pour and drink another cup of firewater. Her senses were beginning to return from her sexual bout with him and she sensed that he would launch another round of abuse against her before he would be able to mount another coital attack. He sat cross legged in front of her, his back against the wall. She trembled as he studied her. "What is he thinking," she asked herself frantically. "When will he be finished with me?"

And then the miracle happened. Slowly, the giant man's eyes began to close. He had just doused himself with another cup of the potent brew. His hand slid down over his vast belly and fell to the floor, letting the little cup roll onto the mat. His chin dropped to his chest. In a moment, Janice heard the unmistakable sound of his snore.

The poor girl began to cry with gratitude. She had been beaten and abused terribly by the trainers and by Tamarov. Ms. Yamamoto had kept her promise and had whipped her until she begged and pleaded for mercy and then gagged her and whipped her some more. But she had always felt that somehow the beatings were instructional. She knew that they fed the lusts of her assailants; she usually had to service them with her mouth or with her lower orifices when they were done. But afterwards, they had bowed to her, she had bowed to them and exchanged polite expressions of gratitude.

But the monster's assault on her had been done for its own sake. He wasn't interested in enlightening her, making her a better whore. He plain old wanted to hurt her for his own amusement. Was this what service outside the training area would be like? Was her world to be filled with men like this huge, cruel, Asian man?

She spent the next hour or more, kneeling before the senseless man, praying that he would never wake. It was her duty to remain where he had left her. It would be a gross violation of rules to move. But after a while, she knelt back, resting her thighs on the back of her shins. She waited, waited, waited. The time dragged slowly. She was hurt and tired, her jaw ached from its distention by her gag.

Janice felt that she had come full circle. She remembered listening to him snore while hanging bound and upside down in her own apartment. Would she ever see that apartment again? What had they done with her clothes, her things? People would have called. Somebody must be aware that she was missing by now. What kind of terrible life was she going to have?

The deeply disturbed girl could not take her eyes off of the slumbering giant. A line of drool ran from the corner of his mouth and his huge belly rose and fell with every breath. What drove this cruel man, she asked herself. Was it hate? Was it just pure meanness? Whatever it was, he had lots of it.

It was after a long while that the man gave a loud snort and jumped to alertness. Janice jumped at the same time, her stomach turning over. She began to tremble as she watched him stir. He looked at her; first with confusion and then with recognition.

Slowly, the man pushed himself to his feet. He walked past the kneeling woman and she heard him lifting the porcelain lid of her chamber pot. He emptied himself into it in a long, steady stream. She dared not turn to look at him. When she heard the lid clink closed, she prepared for the worst. But then she heard the sound of silk sliding against skin. A hand punched the combination lock and she heard the swipe of a card. The lock sprang open and the cruel man left without a word.

* * * * * * * * * * * *

The Budikan Building, housing the banking, commodity trading and various other offices particular to the company's North American enterprises sits on the corner of West 159th Street and Knightsbridge Ave. in he Bronx Cunty, New York. From its offices it is a thirty minute drive to both Kennedy and LaGuardia Airports and about a 20 minute drive to midtown New York, all depending, of course, on the time of day and other traffic conditions. It is a glass enclosed structure and stands 33 stories over the neighboring apartment houses and stores. It is somewhat of an anomaly in the area since most of that section of the Bronx is devoted to residential uses. But when the company began looking for a New York headquarters back in the early 90's, the block on which it sits could be picked up for a song compared to Manhattan real estate.

From Itaki Kuribashi's corner office on the 33rd floor, you could see the boats chugging up and down the Harlem River on the west and the canoes and other paddle craft leisurely cruising the huge Jerome Park Reservoir to the east. At night, the view was spectacular as brilliant lights sparkled everywhere you looked.

Kuribashi had helped pick the location and design the building. On the first through eleventh floors, there were general corporate tenants. The 12th through 32nd floors were all devoted to the Budikan Corporation's business. Since most of the employees came from Japan and were here on short term visits, three floors were allotted to residential use for them. Why pay the exorbitant local rents when you could live in the building virtually rent free? The upper floors' amenities included a karaoke nightclub, a small bowling alley, exercise facilities and a theater.

In between the 27th and 28th floors, the outside of the building was wrapped in a 12' high level of windowless steel. The space in the building that this represented was not set forth on any floor plan. There was no stop on any of the bank of elevators to access it. The only way in and out was an elevator that could be entered only from the deep, cavernous basement of the building, three levels below the street, or from the executive suite.

The executive suite contained, of course, Mr. Kuribashi's office, but it also housed leisure and residential facilities for the dozen or so top executives who worked in the building and for the occasional important visitor from Japan. Hyushu Haruka was one of these. He was young for the responsibilities of his post, only 37. But he was a rising star in the Budikan firmament and had been given an important job to do.

"*You will leave for Nairobi tomorrow?*" Kuribashi asked him. It was evening and the nighttime lights of the largest urban area in the United States presented a stunning background to the executive's lounge. It was on the south side of the building and the shining skyscrapers of

Manhattan covered virtually the whole horizon. The giant window of one way glass ran the length of that side of the building. The room was spacious, well lit and furnished with the finest and most elegant furniture that money could buy.

On the right wall of the room was a bar. A modestly dressed, pretty, young Japanese girl tended it. Around the room the upper management of the New York operation played billiards, chatted or supped together at one of the finely appointed tables. Lithe, elegant young women, dressed in flowing, white and red silk kimonos served them. They were of varied shapes and sizes, and were from different parts of the world. But they all had one thing in common. Etched into their inner thighs they wore the ideograms symbolic of their employer, the Budikan Corporation.

"Yes, at 3 P.M. It's a long flight and that's get me there at about 7 A.M. West African time," Haruka replied.

"Have you made your choice yet?" Kuribashi asked him. He was smoking a long, thick Havana cigar and had a glass of cognac in his hand. He sat opposite the young executive in a plush easy chair. Kuribashi had turned fifty several years ago and had hopes for a high management position back in Kyoto when his New York Stint was done next year. Haruka could be an important ally. Haruka's choice would reflect on him. Kuribashi had recommended the best of the current crop.

"I can't make up my mind between them. I wish I had more time to test them out," the young executive answered. Haruka had arrived from Japan the night before and had spent his day in a whirlwind of meetings. He was looking at a folder containing photographs and background information of Kuribashi's recommendations.

"They'll be up soon and you can see them and make your choice."

* * * * * * * * * * *

Downstairs, on the level between the 'official' 27th and 28th floors, Number Four was getting ready. The matron had instructed her to put on her makeup and to douse herself with the delicate, flowery perfume she had been issued. Janice applied spurts on her neck below the ears, between her breasts and over the plump, hairless lips between her thighs. She painted her finger and toenails a dark maroon to match her lips. When the matron returned she was carrying a red and white, flowered kimono.

The comfort girl trainee had not worn any clothes since her arrival at the company's headquarters and the idea of dressing seemed odd to her. It was a reminder that she had been once used to dressing. Every day, in fact. The silk of the kimono was cool and soft. It covered her to just above her feet and wrapped around her, covering her breasts. The bodice was loose and the sleeves were wide and flowing. The matron proceeded to brush out the girl's long hair and, after gathering it together behind her head, tied the end with a fire engine red silk ribbon that trailed loosely down her back. It could be easily undone with the puling of one end.

Janice stood and watched as the matron applied black, leather clogs to her feet. The matron then took the large mirror that had been placed in Janice's cell and situated it so that the perplexed girl could see her entire body in it. Janice saw the beautiful, pale face of a strange woman. She had lost about ten pounds since she had been recruited and, to her, her face appeared almost gaunt. The kimono bunched around her waist and her hips stood out clearly. She still wore her leather collar and the leather bracelets around her wrists, which seemed quite out of place with the elegant silk robe. She was a comely sight, she had to admit. But to what purpose?

The matron ordered comfort girl trainee Number Four to her knees and had her bend forwards with her breasts crushed against her thighs. The girl had to lift the bottom part of the kimono so that she would not kneel on it. She automatically spread her legs so that access could be had to her sex from behind.

Lifting the back of the kimono, the matron caressed Janice's rear globes gently. The familiar feeling of incipient arousal ran through her. Was this another training exercise, he girl wondered, or was this the real thing? She sensed that she was going to be presented to someone. Was it Mr. Kuribashi, ready to harvest the fruit of her training? Ms. Yamamoto had hinted that someday Mr. Tamarov would take her away. Was that it?

She felt the matron's hand delicately address her naked nether lips and delve a finger lightly along the slit between them. It was not long until the girl gave out a sigh of arousal. The matron leaned over so that she could have Janice's ear. "Number Four very pretty," she whispered in a soft, kind voice. "You see important man, maybe he pick you tonight. Very lucky comfort girl."

Janice tried to take in what the matron was telling her amidst her building lust. Was this the day she was going to be taken away, she wondered nervously. To where? And with whom? What would her life be like? She wanted desperately to leave the oppressive environment of the training areas, but was she going from bad to worse? What kind of man or men would she serve? Would they whip and beat her as relentlessly as she was now?

Her fearful speculations were washed away by a wave of lust that coursed through her as the matron exercised her pleasure bud. Her body was like a finely tuned machine. She could not help but respond passionately to the manipulation of her pleasure organ. "I am a slut, a whore," she thought to herself shamefully. Yet she yearned for the hand to complete its task, to drive her until her whole body shuddered with pleasure.

But, this was not to be. The hand that was firing her lust withdrew, the back of the kimono pulled back down over her pale, round rear globes. The matron ordered her to stand.

Woozy with desire, Janice came to her feet obediently. She felt a hunger in her loins and disappointment at being deprived of the matron's pleasurable caresses. The matron pushed Janice's wrists in front of her and locked them together. She took a long, white sash and, wrapping it around her wrists, pulled the ends together behind her back and tied them off tightly. Janice's hands were pulled close to her body. The matron then presented a large, black rubber ball to Janice's painted lips which the girl allowed her to plop into her mouth. The ball was large enough to still all speech, but not large enough to cause the cheeks to bulge out, distorting her face. On the ball, imprinted on its surface, were the two omnipresent symbols of her 'employer'. Janice winced at the thought that she was carrying the symbols of her enslavement within her mouth.

A golden chain was attached to her collar and the matron pulled down on it until Janice's head was bent down and forward and attached it to her wrists. Janice's attitude was that of a monk at prayer, or, rather, like a dutiful geisha. The last addition to her costume was an 18 inch long chain connecting her ankles together.

The matron stood back. "Pretty, Number Four," she said happily. "You wait," she added. Bowing politely, she left the cell.

Janice stood in place for quite a while. She had no choice; to move without permission was unthinkable. She was used to it. Waiting had been one of the hardest things that she had to learn. When she thought of it, she had spent most of her time waiting. The times of terror and pain and the bouts of mad sexual frenzy had been but interludes between the long periods of uncertainty, discomfort and fear she had experienced locked in her cage or kneeling, hands locked behind her head, in expectancy.

It was Tamarov who came for her. Although her head was bowed down, she knew it was him as soon as he stepped into her cell. He was the only one who came to her, other than her 'clients' of course, who did not wear the uniform kimono of the trainers. He attached a chain to her collar. Wordlessly, he led her out into the hall. Standing there was another young woman, clad identically to her. Janice didn't get an opportunity to see her face, but she saw the leash that had been temporarily tied off to a ring in the wall. Tamarov gathered the other girl's leash and pulled the two prisoners down the hall.

It had been some time since Janice had seen the steel door of the elevator that had brought her to the training areas. It was in a section of the training area that new employees such as her were not taken to. Tamarov pushed the button and the door opened immediately. Before he pushed the button for their destination, he spoke to them.

"Number Four and Number Six, you have had the fortune to be selected as a potential comfort girl to be assigned to a very important person in the Corporation. He will be selecting one of you to go with him to his new post. The one of you who is not selected will be beaten very severely. So I advise you to be your seductive best in his presence."

Janice shivered at the thought of what Tamarov might consider a 'severe' beating. She had suffered at his whip many times. He was cruel and deliberate in the delivery of his strokes. She cast a sideways look at her competition. She could see that she had a shapely form. She tried to remember what Number Six looked like, but it was hard to distinguish between the other trainees without names. She thought that maybe Number Six was the large breasted girl with the sensuous lips and the beautiful face. She had pleasured Janice once and she had been very good indeed. With a sinking feeling in her stomach, Janice hoped that it was not her.

The elevator door slid open at the penthouse floor. Tamarov led the two young women past the receptionist's desk to a door with a coded lock. He put in the combination, swiped his card and the door opened. The girls were taken down another hallway and then through one more locked door.

Janice saw that she had entered a large room and that it was occupied by many people. She felt her leash pulled forwards and she followed, her head bowed, her stride reduced to tiny steps by the chain linking her ankles. She was the picture of a dutiful servant girl. She passed men in business suits sitting in easy chairs, women wearing kimonos similar to hers and heard the low level chatter of a sociable, normal room. When she looked forwards, she could not really look up, she saw, to her amazement, the blazing skyline of New York City. It was night. It was the first time that she knew what time it really was since she had come here. Day and night had lost all meaning to her. She wondered, uneasily, what day it was.

The young woman did not have a long time to speculate. She was brought before a semi-circle of lush, dark brown easy chairs. There were men sitting in each one. Tamarov signaled her to her knees. The other girl knelt down beside her. She felt her collar disconnected from her hands and her chin lifted. Sitting in front of her was a young, well dressed, handsome Japanese man. He looked back at her coolly, as if measuring her desirability. She was sure that he was and, remembering Tamarov's words, she knelt straight erect and pushed out her chest so that her breasts would be well presented. She was kneeling about two feet from the man's legs.

"*They're lovelier in person,*" Haruka noted.

"*Thank you,*" Kuribashi answered, pride in his voice. "*They are both well trained and compliant,*" he continued. "*Let me introduce to you Hans Tamarov. He is the head of procurement and training for this region. I can assure you that you will thank him with every sigh of pleasure for the strict regimen these sluts have undergone. He is a harsh taskmaster.*"

"*Thank you, Kuribashisama,*" Tamarov replied. "*I can tell you, Harukasama that I had great plans for both of these whores. But you will honor me by accepting one of them for your personal use.*"

Haruka had leaned forward in his chair so that he could examine the frightened, young women more closely. He reached out and grabbed their chins and turned their faces right and left. "*No, Tamarov-san, you honor me by presenting me with such a difficult choice. They are both very lovely.*" He looked up at the slavemaster. "*Perhaps I can view their breasts,*" he asked.

"*As you request, Harukasama,*" Tamarov replied. He stepped up to Janice and pulled the kimono down off of her shoulders. Her plump breasts were revealed. He did the same to Number Six.

Haruka seemed impressed by the display of pulchritude. He motioned the two women to come closer to him. Warily, Janice edged herself towards the man until her breasts were almost touching his knee. Number Six did the same. Janice took a sideways look at Number Six's breasts. They were impressive indeed. They were large and firm, with nipples that pointed upwards on their ends. Hers were more round, and smaller. Her heart began to sink.

Haruka took Number Six's breasts in his hands and began to massage them. "*Very pretty,*" he said. "*I could see myself nuzzling these for hours.*" Everyone laughed. He ran his thumbs over the areola and Number Six's nipples obediently stiffened. She smiled coquettishly at the man, although she was just as afraid as Janice. Her real name was Danielle Schuman. She had been recruited much like Janice had, with the introductory letter from a close friend. It had actually come from her cousin. Danielle was a third year student at Colombia University. Her advertisement differed from Janice's in that it promised career advancement, tuition assistance, graduate school admissions. She was on a partial scholarship and her father had just been laid off from a major New York advertising agency. They were going to be unable to pay their share of the $48,000 per year tuition and expenses next year. It had seemed like a godsend. She figured she would scope it out and walk away if it proved to be a scam. She hadn't told anyone that she was going on what she thought was an interview the day after she called. No one had heard from her since.

The executive turned his attention to Janice. He rubbed her breasts as he had Number Six's. "*Firm,*" he said. "*Made for the whip.*"

"*Without a doubt,*" Tamarov interjected.

Janice was trembling as the man caressed her globes. She had tried to manage a smile, but it came off as a grotesque imitation. She cursed herself for her fear. And she cursed herself for wanting this man to choose her. She could not believe that she was actually hoping that this man would want to take her to some unknown destination for an indefinite period of time and use her as his private sex slave. He was handsome, and his hands were gentle and warm. That made it easier. Janice felt the man's thumbs and forefingers grab her thick teats and begin to pinch them. The pressure grew gradually and the man stared at her face for the reaction she would give. The pressure on her nipples very shortly became sharply painful and Janice whined. Her face was a mask of fear.

"*She doesn't like her nipples pinched,*" Haruka remarked, amused. "*Her fear is becoming. Let me see their cunts.*"

Tamarov issued curt orders to the girls and they leaned way back, spreading their legs. Tamarov lifted the fronts of their kimonos up until their upper thighs and the naked, hairless lips between them, were exposed. Haruka noticed the tattoos on their inner thighs with approval. The man caressed their intimacies until they both had begun to lubricate. He gave a hum of satisfaction.

When Janice leaned backwards, her eyes were pointed at the vast floor to ceiling window behind her. Although upside down, she could see the signs of life everywhere. Lights blinked on and off, an airplane passed high overhead. There were people out there who had never heard of the Budikan Corporation, had no inkling of what a 'comfort girl' was. Had no idea that here, in the middle of this 'civilized' city, women were being forced into sexual slavery.

As the hand continued to enflame her, Janice's lust began to build. She knew that her twin tattoos were revealed to the man and she was embarrassed by that knowledge. She couldn't image ever getting used to it. But then, she had gotten used to a lot of things recently that she would have thought that she wouldn't have.

The unseen hand began to tickle her hardened clit and the comfort girl candidate moaned. Number Six followed suit shortly thereafter. The hand was withdrawn. Tamarov ordered the girls to turn and bend over. Janice felt the back of her kimono being lifted. Hands caressed her rear globes.

Haruka sat back in his chair. "*Kuribasha-san, you have presented me with a real dilemma.*" He motioned for one of the comfort girl waitresses to bring him another drink. 24 year old single malt scotch was his beverage of choice and the waitress delivered it neat with a side of cool, clear water. He motioned to Tamarov to take the empty chair to his right. "*Please sit and have a drink, Tamarov-san. You deserve it.*"

Tamarov nodded his assent and thanks and sat in the large, comfortable chair. Kuribashi was nursing a martini. Tamarov ordered a Jack Daniels on the rocks.

The men chatted happily as the two women knelt before them, their pale, white half moons presented, their dainty little brown stars exposed. Some of the other executives wandered over from time to time and introduced themselves to Haruka, who might one day might be their boss, and to admire the exposed intimacies of the two women. Janice could hear the men gather around and she could sense the women coming and going delivering drinks and hors d'oeurves. How many of them, she wondered, had knelt like this waiting for judgment? What did they think of her obsequious obedience?

Kuribashi made a suggestion to Haruka, one that was immediately seized by all as an amusing solution to his dilemma. *"Let's have two of the other sluts lick their cunts until they come. The one who comes first wins."*

Haruka smiled and agreed. It appealed to his sporting nature. Also, fate played a heavy role in his world outlook and leaving the choice to fate seemed appropriate. He really couldn't complain regardless of which one he took.

Janice and the other girl were ordered to lie on the backs and to spread their legs. Kuribashi gave two waitresses instructions in English. Although most of the comfort girls who served here were from abroad, English was the 'lingua franca' when dealing with them. There was no interest in teaching them Japanese beyond the rudimentary knowledge they needed to perform their tasks.

Janice did not know that she was in a contest. If she had, she would probably have frozen up. She felt a waitress kneel next to her, her head towards her feet, lean over and begin to caress her sex. Janice figured that the man wanted a display of lasciviousness and she vowed to give him a show. But she was wrong when she assumed that she should last as long as possible before letting the female tongue push her past the barrier to her pleasure.

When the woman's warm mouth settled on her delicate lower lips, Janice moaned. She cursed herself for her wantonness. She had closed her eyes, but she sensed and heard the crowd of men who had assembled around the sporting Sapphic display. The woman's hands danced across her sensitive thighs and her tongue traced a line down her slit. Janice felt her consciousness cloud as she experienced the warmth of arousal. Janice had only been a comfort girl for a little over two months, but the women who was teasing her hard clit with the tip of her tongue had been one for considerably longer. She knew that it was in her interest to provide the men with a memorable show. She didn't know the parameters of the contest, but she knew that her own abilities were on display. Like most of the girls, she knew the benefits of being selected as the private comfort girl of a high executive rather than being a commonly held slut. Maybe one of the men would select her some day soon.

Haruka watched the pair of girls respond to the attentions of the waitresses. Their mouths were parted and their exposed breasts had hardened. Little things meant much to him, and he admired how the toes of the big breasted girl curled as her lust was driven onwards. He saw Janice's eyes flutter as her assailant gave her pussy an oral massage.

The skilled waitresses had both drawn up the rear of their kimonos so that their charms would be also on display. There would be passionate reverberations from their activities and they both stood to be its beneficiaries.

The room was silent except for the moans of the two fledgling comfort girls. Janice began to squirm and her back arched as the teasing of the tongue on her bud became almost unbearable. Her blood was rushing in her ears; her heart was pumping wildly. She felt the familiar sensation of her orgasm building. "No! No! No!" she tried to call, but the sinister black ball in her mouth suppressed her words. She felt that all eyes were on her oozing canal as the woman pressed her thighs wide apart and leaned away to let her passions cool. She felt the men's eyes pierce her gushing, dilated sex. The experienced woman gently teased the open wound with her hand and then, again, brought her skilled mouth to bear.

As the tongue began to enflame her anew, Janice was unable to hold back any longer. Her body spasmed as the hard contractions of her pussy's walls came again and again. She moaned loudly; her bound hands strained at their confinement.

The group of men burst into a cheer. There was laughter all around as money changed hands. Haruka smiled. The choice had been made.

The orgasm of the other candidate was anticlimactic. Janice heard her howl and moan even as her own contractions began to diminish. Janice thought that all was lost. The other girl had proved to be a better spectacle. Her mind filled with terror at the punishment that awaited her.

But when the two new comfort girls were brought back to their knees, it was the other girl who had the leash reattached to her collar. She must have understood at once what it meant, because she whined with fear and dismay. Tamarov led her away without further ado. It hit Janice all at once that she had sealed her own fate. She looked up into the hard eyes of her new master. Should she be happy or should she be afraid? There was no way to tell.

Kuribashi grinned happily. He was sure that Haruka would not soon forget this evening's entertainment.

After the men had dispersed, Janice remained kneeling before the man to whom she now belonged. He looked at her with cold, assessing eyes. Her face and chest with still flushed with evidence of her passion. Her bare breasts still hung invitingly outside of her kimono. She saw the man free his already hardened cock from his pants. She did not need to be told what to do. She crept up between his legs and captured the hard flesh between her lips.

As the bulbous head passed over her tongue, sliding across the roof of her mouth, Janice wondered how many times she would be in a similar position; how many times would she have to service this handsome man's desires. She felt grateful for being chosen by him. She communicated her gratitude with her lips and her tongue. Slowly, deliberately, she brought the man to pleasure. She thrilled to hear him sigh and moan as she teased the underside of his manhood's helmeted head with her tongue. When he groaned as she pushed her head deep into his lap, taking all of his length within her, she reveled in her skill. When he discharged into her mouth, she received it with joy.

* * * * * * * * * * *

Janice spent the night in the bed of her new master. When she was naked and kneeling on all fours on the mattress, he gave her five strong strokes with a cane. Although the blows were painful, Janice received them as her due and obediently counted off the blows in Japanese as she had been taught. He ravished her fore and aft, filling her with his long, thick, steel hard rod. For the first time since her induction into this strange world she now belonged to, she slept in the arms of a man.

In the morning, she was taken back down to her cell. Her trainer awaited her. She was given a final set of instructions. Later, when he returned, Janice held up to him a handwritten note and an addressed envelope. Two hours later, a bound and gagged young woman, wearing the red and white kimono of her new station in life, was led aboard a large private jet bearing the name and insignias of the Budikan Corporation. Soon after that, it was in the air.

* * * * * * * * * * *

A few days later, on the west side of Chicago, a pretty, young woman trudged up the stairs of her three storey walkup. It had been another stressful and unrewarding day at the law firm of Pilkins, Dieter and Grabowski. She was a receptionist on the third floor of the firm's downtown five floor Chicago offices. She had been there for two years. She had just about had enough.

The shapely, young woman carried with her that day's mail which she had drawn from her mailbox on the ground floor. She dumped her purse on the stand near the door and then dumped the mail on the kitchen table. She was anxious to get out of her tight, stifling skirt and her stylish but uncomfortable high heels. Standing in the kitchen, garbed in only her lacey, black panties and her matching bra, she downed a mouthful of scotch. The warmth of the alcohol spread through her body and she began to feel relaxed.

There were only two things of note in her mail: a letter from her friend, Janice, and a large manila envelope labeled 'Open Immediately' in big, red letters. She tossed the big envelope aside and read her friend's letter. It was terse but friendly. When she finished it, she took another look at the larger envelope and, after a moment's hesitation, opened it. There was a colorful brochure in it promising to change her life. It seemed too good to be true. But it had been a horrible day after a long string of horrible days at work. She thought for a moment and then thought, "Why not?" She picked up the phone and dialed.

The End